DONN McCLEAN is a sports writer, specialising in horse racing. He is chief racing writer for *The Sunday Times* in Ireland and he writes a weekly column for *The Irish Field*. A three-time nominee for the HWPA Racing Writer of the Year award, he has also ghost-written four racing autobiographies.

Winner of a Louth under-21 championship medal with his club, the O'Connells, when he was sixteen, Donn now lives with his wife and four daughters in Wicklow, where he coaches his daughter's under-14 soccer team. This is his first book for younger readers.

DONN McCLEAN

THE O'BRIEN PRESS
DUBLIN

First published 2020 by
The O'Brien Press Ltd,
12 Terenure Road East, Rathgar,
Dublin 6, Ireland
D06 HD27
Tel: +353 1 4923333; Fax: +353 1 4922777
E-mail: books@obrien.ie
Website: www.obrien.ie
The O'Brien Press is a member of Publishing Ireland.

ISBN: 978-1-78849-183-9

8 7 6 5 4 3 2 1
23 22 21 20

Printed and bound by ScandBook in the EU.
The paper in this book is produced using pulp from managed forests.

Published in:

DUBLIN
UNESCO
City of Literature

MIX
Paper from
responsible sources
FSC® C021394

DEDICATION

To my favourite girls' team:
Rachel, Annie, Ella, Maggie and Kitty. (No subs.)

ACKNOWLEDGEMENTS

Big thanks to all the people whose input was willingly given,
including Marie Crowe, John Greene, Diarmuid O'Boyle, Ella
O'Reilly and Julie Rose O'Brien. And to Daragh Ó Conchúir
for his expert advice.
Míle buíochas.

Thanks to Lily for taking the time to write this book's first
review. To Michael O'Brien for his unwavering support; to
Emma Byrne for the care and time she took in the design of the
cover; to Brenda Boyne for her continued help, and to Helen
Carr, for her unfailing enthusiasm and her fantastic attention to
detail.

And to Dad. For all the support and for everything.

Chapter 1

SUMMER SHOWERS

Summer showers, they had said. Maybe some summer showers. They didn't say that it would rain all day.

And it was lashing. The middle of August, and it was lashing. No relenting. I was soaking wet. I was certain that I had never been as wet in my life. I zipped my coat up to the very top so that I could feel the cold, sharp zip against my neck, and I pulled the peak of my hood down as far over my forehead as I could. Even so, my head was wet. Soaked. My whole body was wet. And cold. I closed my eyes and imagined that I was sitting at home by the fire with my hands wrapped around a mug of hot chocolate.

I only opened my eyes because someone beside me shouted.

'Go on, Tina!'

Tina had the ball and was going on one of her solo runs. She was well past the 45 and she was heading for the 21. One of the Castleherron girls was marking her, harrying her, grabbing at her, trying to stop her or at least slow her down, but Tina was strong. She could have picked up the Castleherron girl and carried her. When she got inside the 21 she fell to the ground and the Castleherron girl fell on top of her. The whistle blew. Free in.

Tina picked herself up slowly.

'Are you okay Tina?' Stephen shouted beside me in the dugout.

Tina didn't answer. Of course she was okay. Tina was always okay. She just acted like she wasn't okay sometimes. When she needed a little bit of attention.

Shelley went over to her, maybe to ask her if she was okay, maybe to offer to take the free kick if Tina didn't feel up to it. But Tina was up to it all right. Even if her leg had been hanging off, Tina wasn't going to let anyone else take that free kick.

She poked her foot into the ground to make an imaginary hole at the spot at which she had been fouled. Ball in her hands, she took two steps back. Then she took another step back. Then another. It was her routine. She must have learned it from rugby. Apparently she was a good rugby player too. In truth, she didn't need all the ceremony. She was no more than 15 metres from the goals. A strong gust of wind would have blown the ball over the bar from there.

She took her four steps forwards, a walk first, then a jog, and kicked. The ball left her right boot and sailed high and straight over the bar. Right over the black spot.

'Brilliant, Tina!' shouted Stephen beside me, clapping his hands together. 'Well done.'

That was the insurance point. It put us four points ahead and there were only about five minutes left. Even if Castleherron scored a goal now, we would still be a point ahead. Four points is a good lead.

'Anna,' said Stephen urgently, barely glancing in my direction. 'Get ready.'

Get ready? Five minutes to go and I was soaking wet and freezing cold. Usually, you're dying to get on. You're dying to play. In fact, I was disappointed that I hadn't started. I couldn't realistically have expected to start, I had only just joined the team after all. But even so. I was still a bit disappointed that I wasn't in the starting fifteen.

But to go on now as a sub? With five minutes to go? In the rain? I wasn't sure that I would even be able to take my coat off.

'Come on, Anna,' said Stephen sharply. 'Hurry up.'

I put in my gum shield and I managed to unzip my coat slowly with my wet fingers as the other subs looked at me, probably with a mixture of jealousy and relief. Jealousy that I had been chosen in front of them to go on, relief that they didn't have to de-robe and leave the semi-shelter of the dugout.

'Ref!' shouted Stephen, as he rolled his hands around to indicate a substitution. The ref blew his whistle and held up his hand, to stop the Castleherron goalkeeper before she kicked the ball out.

'You're going on left half-forward, okay?'

I nodded.

'Michelle!' Stephen shouted, and Shelley came trotting over towards us. 'Go on, Anna,' said Stephen. 'Do your best.'

I went to touch hands with Shelley as we passed each other, me going on, she coming off. I thought it was what subs did. But Shelley didn't touch hands. She just ran straight past me. She didn't even look at me.

Suit yourself Shelley.

I got into my position, left half-forward, beside the number five from Castleherron. I looked at the Castleherron goalkeeper as she lined up her kick-out. I looked beyond her goals, but there was nobody there. There was never anybody behind the opposition's goals. Nobody of note anyway. Not any more.

Suddenly I felt a sharp pain in my shoulder and I went flying. My feet actually left the ground. I wasn't expecting the shoulder from the number five. I wasn't braced, I was off balance. Before I really knew what was happening, I was lying on the ground with a sore shoulder. I could only watch with a worm's-eye view as the ball came my way. The Castleherron number five caught it, uncontested, and kicked it down the field towards our goal.

'Anna, for God's sake,' said Tina as she turned and ran back towards our goal.

'Come on, Anna!' I could hear Stephen's voice. It had more disappointment in it than encouragement.

I picked myself up. Mucky as well as wet now. It should have been a free. You can't shoulder. The ref should have been watching. I should have been awarded a free in. I watched as Castleherron went down and scored a point. Only three in it now.

Sofia kicked the ball out. Sofia was a good goalkeeper, but she didn't have a very strong kick. She kicked the ball towards Debbie, but the Castleherron number seven was stronger. She caught the ball in front of Debbie, bounced it once, soloed it once, and kicked it over the bar.

'Come on Ballymarra!'

I could hear the frustration in Stephen's voice. He was standing on the sideline, miles away from the dugout.

Now it was worrying. We were only two points ahead. If Castleherron scored a goal, they would win by a point and put us out of the championship. They nearly did as well. They won Sofia's next kick-out and attacked again. Their number nine, their best player, passed it to their number 13. She was clear in on goal, she only had Sofia to beat, but she hit it too high and it went over the bar as Sofia dived to the ground.

It wasn't a goal, but was a point and it left us just one point ahead.

Sofia got the ball and kicked it out. While it was in the air, before Tina jumped and tried to catch it, the referee blew his whistle. Two sharp blasts and one long one – phewp, phewp, pheeeeeewwwwwwwp – that signalled the end of the match.

There was a quiet cheer. People clapped. Tina punched the air.

I was glad that it was over. I hadn't even touched the ball in the four or five minutes that I had been on the pitch, but I didn't care. I was relieved. I was relieved that we had won, I was relieved that my mistake hadn't been a factor in us losing the match but, if I was being honest with myself, I was more relieved that I was able to get back to the relative warmth of the dressing room.

Chapter 2

GRANNY AND GRANDAD

It was warm and dry in Granny and Grandad's kitchen, but I was still cold. I sat there in my pyjamas and my dressing gown, all bundled up, still trying to warm up. The shower in Granny and Grandad's is never as strong or as hot as you would like it to be.

Granny and Grandad are great, though. I love them very much. I probably love Granny a little more than I love Grandad, but I'd never say that to anyone. Not even to Granny, and not even to Mum. Definitely not to Mum.

Grandad is very nice and he is very good to me and Charlie. He tells us jokes and he does magic tricks. But he gets a little bit cross sometimes. Like if you tap the back of his newspaper while he is reading it. Granny never gets cross. She's always smiling, even when she is sad, and she hugs us lots.

She hugged us lots and lots when we moved in with them during the summer. That was just over a year after the worst summer in the world.

Chapter 3

THE WORST SUMMER

The worst summer in the world was the summer we lost Daddy. That's what Mum says. 'We lost Dad.'

Actually, he died. I find it easier to say that he died, because that's what happened. We didn't lose him. Daddy died. I remember that day. I remember everything about that day. I'll never forget that terrible, terrible day.

He came into my room that morning as he always did in the morning. He kissed me on the head and said, 'Good morning, chicken'. I was usually awake before he came into me, but I was asleep that day. I stretched my arm up and put it around his neck. I wasn't awake enough to speak, but I was awake enough to hug him. I was always awake enough to hug Daddy.

I said what in my head was, 'Morning, Daddy', but it came out as something like 'Muffeldonken'. I pressed my head against his head though, my face against his face. His face was always prickly, but I didn't mind. I loved the prickles on his face. I could feel him smiling.

He hugged me back for a few minutes. Not long enough. It was never long enough and it definitely wasn't long enough that morning. Then he kissed me on the side of the head, just above my ear.

'What's going on with you today, chicken?' he said.

He always called me chicken and in the morning he always asked me what was going on with me today. I wasn't awake enough to remember my name or my dreams, but I did remember that Sally was coming around. Sally always came around.

'Sally's coming around,' I managed to say.

Daddy smiled.

'Of course she is,' he said. 'Tell Sally Cat that I said hello.'

Daddy called Sally 'Sally Cat'. It was a play on 'alley cat', I guess. They had this thing. When Daddy would see Sally, he'd say, hello Sally Cat. Every time. And she'd say 'Hello, Jack Cat'. That was a play on nothing. It was just something that Sally called Daddy, because he called her Sally Cat. Their little exchanges always made me smile.

'And tomorrow?' he asked.

I was beginning to wake up properly. I could see his smiling face in the half-light, and my brain started to click into working mode. Tomorrow, I thought. What's happening tomorrow?

'County trials!' I blurted out, almost before the thought had finished formulating in my head.

Daddy reached down and picked something up from my bedroom floor. I could hear the crinkling of paper before I saw what was in his hand. Brown paper wrapping, Sellotaped together very badly. He put the package on the bed beside me.

'What's that?' I asked.

I didn't know what it was, but I knew that it was for me and I couldn't stop smiling.

'Only one way to find out,' said Daddy.

I unstuck the badly stuck Sellotape carefully and opened the package. Inside the brown-paper package was something wrapped in cellophane. I couldn't make it out at first. It was soft inside the cellophane. Soft and squidgy. And orange.

I love orange. I love everything orange.

'Football socks!' I exclaimed. 'Luminous orange football socks!' I flung my arms around him. 'Thank you Daddy!'

'You're very welcome chicken.'

I opened the package and took out the socks. I pulled them apart so that I had one of them in my left hand and the other in my right hand.

'Now, the thing about those socks,' said Daddy softly. 'Of course, they will make you play the best football that you have ever played in your entire life. But, more importantly for tomorrow, they will also make you stand out. When the county selectors are watching you, you won't just be the girl with the black curly hair. You will be the girl in the orange socks.'

I flung my arms around him again. I just clung to him. His prickly face against my cheek. The clean fresh smell of his skin. I loved the smell of Daddy's skin.

'I probably won't get picked,' I said.

Daddy pulled his head back and looked at me, smiling, a hint of surprise in his eyes.

'I'm only twelve,' I explained. 'It's under-14s. For the county.'

'Listen chicken,' said Daddy softly. 'You have done brilliantly to get picked for the trials. And, you're right, you are young, but they wouldn't have picked you for the trials if they didn't think that you had a chance of making the panel. Just do your best. That's all you can do. I know you will.'

'Will you be there? You don't have to work do you?'

'I wouldn't miss it!'

I hugged him again.

'So what's going on with you today, Daddy?' I asked eventually, as I carefully folded the socks and put them back into their plastic package.

'I'm on site,' he said. 'I'm in the office first thing, then I have to go to that site in Ballybrit for a few hours. But I should be home for dinner. And we can go out and play football on the green this evening after dinner if you want.'

I did want. I always wanted to play football with Daddy. Nobody could kick the ball as high as Daddy could kick the ball.

It was just a normal summer's day for most people, a normal summer Friday, and it would have been a normal summer's day for me too. I wish it had been just a normal summer's day for me. I wish that more than I wish for anything in the world. I wish that there was no reason why I should remember the details of the day like I remember them. I only remember the details because of what happened.

I wore my white shorts and my Adidas t-shirt and my baby-blue flip-flops. Sally came around at about eleven o'clock, and we just hung out in my room, chatting.

We could chat for hours. About nothing and everything. Clothes and hair and climbing trees and the girls in school and our little brothers, Alan and Charlie, about how annoying or cute they were, depending on your perspective. Miss Ferguson and the other teachers and Mrs Moloney who lived in number 26 and boys. Sally had a crush on William. William was nice, but he was too pretty for me. I liked Freddie a little bit. He was quiet and his hair was always messy, but he was always kind to everybody, even to Miss Ferguson, and he had a nice face. Nobody knew that I liked him except Sally. I didn't go on about it that much. Sally liked William way more than I liked Freddie.

It was at 12.32 that the doorbell rang and I heard the voices in the hall. I knew that it was 12.32, because I looked at my clock. It sounded like Sally's mum, and it sounded like people were crying. Sally and I went out of my bedroom and went to the top of the stairs.

'Mum?' I called.

No answer. I looked at Sally. She looked worried.

'Mum?' I called again.

'Yes, pet,' she answered. Sniffly. 'Come down, pet. Come down here.'

I went down the stairs slowly with Sally just behind me. Something felt off. Mum and Sally's mum were in the hall. They both had tears streaming down their faces.

'What's wrong, Mum?'

She just grabbed me and hugged me and started crying again. I could feel her whole body shaking and I could hear her crying. I had never heard Mum crying before. I had seen her cry at movies and stuff, but she would cry silently. You wouldn't know that she was crying unless you looked at her face. This was different though. This was not crying at movies crying.

I started crying. I didn't know what I was crying about. I was crying for Mum, but I was also scared about why she was crying. Sally's mum hugged the two of us and Sally hugged me. Sally started to cry. We all stood there in the hall, hugging and crying and I didn't know why.

Finally, Mum pulled away from my hug, and she lowered her face to mine, so that I could see the red that was in her eyes behind her tears.

'Dad has had an accident at work,' she said.

'Is he okay?' I managed to ask just before I burst into

tears again.

Mum grabbed me and hugged me again.

'I don't know, pet,' she said through her tears. 'I have to go to the hospital now. You and Charlie go with Sally and Brenda. You can stay in Brenda's house for the afternoon.'

'Are you sure that you don't want me to come with you?' asked Sally's mum.

'No, Brenda,' said Mum. 'Thanks for taking the kids. I don't know what time ...'

'Of course,' said Sally's mum.

She grabbed Mum's two hands with her two hands.

Charlie came out of the sitting room, clutching his bunny. Big sleepy head on him.

'I'm hungry, Mummy,' he said.

☣ ☣ ☣

That was the worst afternoon that I have ever had. The worst afternoon that anyone has ever had, I'd say. We stayed in Sally's room and I cried lots. Sally hugged me lots. Even Alan, her annoying little brother, came in and gave me a hug. Sally and I tried to play Monopoly, but we didn't really succeed. Sally bought Park Lane and Mayfair, and I didn't care.

'Poor Daddy,' I remember thinking all through that afternoon. It must have been a bad accident if Mum was so upset. He must have been hurt badly. Badly enough to have to go to hospital. I couldn't wait to see him and hug him.

I remembered when Alice Conway fell in yard and broke her arm. She had to go to hospital. It seemed like she was in a lot of pain. She cried and cried all the way from the yard to Mrs Scally's car, and probably all the way to the hospital in Mrs Scally's car.

Daddy dying was the last thing on my mind. I didn't even consider it. Looking back now, of course I should have. He was killed in the accident. Nobody told me the details, but I overheard people talking at the funeral. Adults sometimes forget that kids have ears.

He was high up in the air. He was climbing on some scaffolding and he fell. I don't know why he was climbing on scaffolding. I didn't know what scaffolding was before then, and I didn't know that architects climbed on it. And I don't know how he fell. He just did. That's what happened. It doesn't matter why or how anyway. It doesn't change the fact that Daddy is not here anymore.

I cried non-stop for days. I went to bed crying, and I got up crying. I didn't do anything else. I didn't want to do anything else. I didn't go to the county trials the following day and I didn't wear the luminous orange football socks that Daddy had bought for me. I didn't even take them back out of their plastic package. I threw them into the bottom of my wardrobe and left them there. I didn't want to be reminded of the last time that I saw Daddy.

I didn't want to play football and I didn't want to ride my bike and I didn't want to play Minecraft with Sally. Sally came around lots and I just cried with her. I was sad all the time. I lost weight and Mum worried.

I had stopped the non-stop crying by the time I went back to school that September, into sixth class. But I was still sad. I cried nearly every day. The teachers were nice to me and my friends were nice to me, but it didn't help. Patricia Kelly was mean to me, but Patricia Kelly was always mean to me, and I cared less about it that September than I had ever cared about it in my life before.

'Your dad wasn't as good as my dad anyway,' she said to me one day.

I just kicked her on the shin and she ran away crying.

I was up in Mrs Scally's office for that, but Mrs Scally let me off with just a warning.

Chapter 4

• • • • •

LIVING WITH GRANNY AND GRANDAD

'Here you go love,' said Granny, as she handed me a cup of steaming hot chocolate and smiled. Granny always calls me love.

I wrapped my fingers around the cup. Thanks Granny. She's the best. The cup was almost too hot for my hands, but it was just about bearable. I gripped it tightly and took a sip. I held the warm chocolate in my mouth for a few seconds before I swallowed it. This was a Granny special. Extra chocolate.

It wasn't that I didn't like living with Granny and

Grandad. I loved that I was getting to spend lots of time with them. When we were living in Galway, we didn't see them very often. We only got to see them at holiday time, Christmas and Easter and summer, and sometimes on long weekends. It always felt like a long drive from Galway to Wicklow, from Mountbridge to Ballymarra, and Charlie usually got sick somewhere along the way.

Granny and Grandad came to stay with us in Galway for a while shortly after Daddy died. I liked having them there. Granny was no substitute for Daddy, but she was warm and comforting and she understood it when I started to cry for no apparent reason. Grandad went back to Wicklow after a week or two, but Granny stayed for the whole summer.

I didn't play football that summer. I didn't kick a ball. I didn't feel up to it. I didn't feel up to much. I missed all the county trials, but I didn't care.

I didn't care about much really. I wandered around listlessly, aimlessly. Some nights I watched television and some nights I didn't. Some nights I cried myself to sleep and some nights I didn't cry and some nights I didn't sleep.

Mum took us away for Christmas. It was weird, Christmas in the Canary Islands, in the sun. It was very hard too, Christmas without Daddy, but it was a good idea to go away. Christmas at home without Daddy would have been unbearable.

The team started training in early February. I didn't go back initially. I wasn't sure how I would feel. Without Daddy there, you know.

Daddy used to go to my games. Almost all my games. He hardly missed one. It didn't matter where the game was or when it was. Weekend games, weekday games. He always made it his business to be there. I'm not sure how he managed it. He must have arranged his work schedule around my games. Games in Clifden, games in Portumna, games in Ballymoe. It didn't matter.

He always stood behind the goals that we were attacking. I could always see the delight on his face when I did something good. A good pass or a good tackle or a good block. I always looked for his reaction when I could. I always saw the delight on his face when we scored, when any of the girls scored, and that delight was heightened if I scored. And I could always see his claps and hear his shouts of encouragement if I missed.

He never gave out. He never criticised. He always encouraged. He always pointed out what we were doing right, not what we were doing wrong.

On the rare occasions when he wasn't there, I felt that something was missing. It wasn't that I didn't feel motivated, I always did my best anyway. But when Daddy was there, I just felt more confident. The ball would bounce for me. I felt that I could anticipate where the ball was going to break. The girls would give me the passes that I wanted. My shots would go just inside the post instead of just outside the post.

I couldn't imagine going back playing, knowing that Daddy wasn't going to be there. Knowing that he wouldn't be there again. Ever.

Mum said it to me one evening during the summer, about maybe starting back training, that it might be good for me. But I didn't think so. I wasn't ready. I thought that I was getting there, but I didn't think that I was ready. Mum didn't push it.

I met the under-14s manager, Eamonn Doherty, in the shop the following week, and he asked me if I was coming back. He said that I would be a big addition to the team. I said I didn't know.

A few days later, I got home from Sally's house and he was in the kitchen, having a cup of tea with Mum.

'Hi, pet,' said Mum. 'How was your day?'

'It was okay,' I said.

Okay was as good as days got.

'Hi Anna,' said Eamonn.

'Eamonn has just been talking to me about the team

this year,' said Mum. 'It's a big year for the team, it's a big year for the club. You know it could be a very good team this year. All the girls. Eamonn says that you would have a real chance of winning the county championship. No girls' team from the club has ever won a county championship before. Did you know that?'

'I did,' I said simply.

Eamonn wasn't saying much.

'He would love if you would play,' continued Mum. 'He says that they have a strong team anyway but, with you, it would be even stronger.'

'Okay,' I said.

They were both a bit taken aback.

'Okay?' said Eamonn, a bit hesitantly. 'Okay, you'll play?'

'Yep,' I said.

I missed playing. I missed the girls. Even the older girls. Jess and Lucy and Nancy and Caoimhe. Sally was usually a sub, but she was still a part of it all. I missed playing with them.

'That's great, Anna,' said Eamonn. 'Really great.'

He stood up and I thought he was going to hug me but, if he was, he stopped himself. He gave me this awkward pat on the shoulder, then an even more awkward pat on the other shoulder.

'I know how tough a time it has been for you,' he said. He didn't know. He couldn't have known. But I knew that he meant it well. 'It could be very good for you to come back. The girls will be so happy.'

It wasn't as difficult as I thought it was going to be, going back to that first training session. It actually felt good to be back. The girls were great, and the drills were not that difficult. Most of all though, it felt good to be back on a football pitch with a ball in my hands and my team mates around me. I trained hard that night and I came home exhausted.

My first match back was difficult though. Daddy rarely went to training. A match was different.

I didn't cry in the dressing room before the match. I held it together in front of the girls. As soon as we got outside though, I broke down. I had to go behind the dressing room as all the other girls went out onto the pitch, and I bawled my eyes out.

I played terribly. I started in midfield, I was moved to full-forward at half time, and Eamonn took me off with ten minutes to go. I was annoyed at the time, but I knew that he was right to take me off. I was awful.

I knew that Daddy wasn't there of course. I knew that he wasn't going to be there. But I kept looking for him. Behind the goals.

A few minutes into that match, I thought I heard his voice and I looked. Then a few minutes later, I thought I heard his voice again, and I looked again. I must have looked for him about a hundred times. My mind wasn't on the game.

We lost that match. We didn't lose by much, just two points, 2-8 to 1-9, but it was a match that we shouldn't have lost. We always beat Tubberkerrin.

We didn't win the championship that year either. We got a little bit better later in the summer, we got to the quarter-final, but Drumcrogan hockeyed us in that, and they went on to win the final.

It was a pity. It was a big achievement to get to the quarter-final, but we all felt that it was one that got away. We had the team to win the championship. We just didn't play to our potential.

I was miles away from my best. I struggled with everything. My timing was off, my passing was poor, my shooting was really bad. I had some good spells in one or two matches, I scored some points and I scored one goal, but I didn't play well. In truth, I didn't have one good game. I cried before some games and I nearly cried before all the others.

I didn't admit it to anyone, not even to Sally, but I wasn't that disappointed when we lost the quarter-final. A county championship medal would have been nice, but the pain might have been unbearable. The only thing I would have wanted to do with that medal would have been to share it with Daddy.

And I mightn't even have been there for the semi-final or the final. We were moving.

Chapter 5

NEW GIRL

I didn't want to move. I had my friends in Mount-bridge. I had my school, I knew the teachers, I knew where I was going to secondary school: to St Vincent's with Sally and Kate and Evelyn and Hannah.

Mum had been talking about it for a little while though. Mountbridge was Dad's home, she told me. All her friends in Mountbridge were actually Dad's friends. They were all great in the beginning, we had lots of people calling around to us in the first few weeks after Daddy died. In the first few months.

But it was a very couplesy community, Mum told me. That means that people hang out in couples, she said, not as singles and not in big groups. Everybody was in a couple. If you weren't in a couple, you stood out. Mum used to go to things on her own in the beginning, but she didn't enjoy being there without Daddy. She always felt that people would invite her to things out of pity. When people would speak to her, they would speak to her with this sad, pitiful voice, and they would talk about Daddy. About how great he was. About how well she was coping. After they had finished talking about all of that, she said, they would run out of things to talk about.

She said that her only true friend in Mountbridge was Brenda, Sally's mum.

Mum wasn't a local, she told me. She hadn't been born and bred in Mountbridge. And that was a big thing. As time went on, she said that she realised she didn't have much in common with a lot of the people she had considered to be her friends. As more time went on, she stopped going to things. And as she stopped going to things, people stopped inviting her to things.

She wasn't working either, and that was another big thing, she told me. Her job had been with Daddy, in Daddy's business. It was just the two of them. Without Daddy, she said, there was no business.

The insurance money wouldn't last forever, she said,

so she would have to go and get a job at some stage anyway, and there weren't many jobs in Mountbridge. One of her childhood friends, Denise Maguire, had a small design business in Mum's home village in Ballymarra in County Wicklow, and she had told Mum that there was a job for her there whenever she wanted it.

Mum said that she dismissed it out of hand in the beginning, but the more time moved on, and the more Denise said it to her, and the more out of place she felt in Mountbridge, the more sense a move to Ballymarra seemed to make.

We were a big factor in her decision, she said. Charlie and me. She didn't want to uproot us, move us away from our friends. Move me away from my football. But we were young, she said. We could make new friends. And I could join the Ballymarra football team.

And if there was a good time to do it, it was after I finished primary school, before I started secondary school, so that I wouldn't be joining secondary school in the middle of a year. So that I wouldn't always be known as the new girl.

Gradually the realisation dawned on me that we were definitely moving. I was resigned to that reality. I didn't really want to leave Mountbridge, I didn't want to leave Sally and my friends.

Sally was brilliant. She was just there for me. She was happy to do whatever I wanted to do, and she was happy to just sit with me in silence if I didn't want to speak. And she knew when to hug me and when to leave me alone. She knew when I cried needing a hug and she knew when I cried needing to be left alone. She knew that better than I knew it.

And Kate was great. Evelyn would never call around to me without Kate, but Kate often came without Evelyn. I can't have been great company, but they still kept calling for me, seeing if I wanted to go out or if I just wanted to sit in, and they were happy enough if I just wanted to be left alone.

I didn't want to leave them. I didn't want to move to a new place where I knew nobody. But I didn't protest too much. I guess I was a bit numb about the whole idea. I was numb about everything really. And at least it would be a new start, I thought. It might help me not feel so sad.

Mum bought one of the new houses that were being built just outside Ballymarra. It wasn't ready in August, but Mum wanted us to move a few weeks before school started, get settled into the community well before I started secondary school, so we moved in with Granny and Grandad at the start of August. Just for a few months, Mum said.

I remember the evening that Mum told me that we were moving.

'I have good news and bad news,' she said.

That's rarely good. The bad news is usually more 'bad' than the good news is 'good'.

'What's the bad news?' I asked.

I always wanted the bad news first.

'How about the good news first this time?' asked Mum, smiling.

Sometimes you have to give the good news first. I realise that. Like, if the bad news is related to the good news. I remember when Daddy bought me my new bike, he said to me, I have good news and I have bad news. I insisted on hearing the bad news first. He said, it's not orange.

'Okay,' I said to Mum.

'Right,' Mum said. 'The good news is that Ballymarra have a really good set up for girls' football, and that they have a girls' under-14 team. I have all the forms here. Transfer forms and registration forms and everything.'

She put her hands up in the air, smiling, and mouthed the word 'Yay!' without saying it.

I smiled. That was indeed good news.

'And the bad news?' I asked.

'Oh yes, the bad news,' she said, looking a little wor-ried.

'I went to school with the manager, Stephen Kane, and he's very nice.'

She squished up her face and her nose. I was a bit puzzled.

'That's not bad news,' I said. 'Is it?'

'No, I guess it's not,' she said. 'That's actually good news. So two pieces of good news then.'

Chapter 6

• • • • •

TRAINING

I went to my first training session with Ballymarra two days after we moved. That was difficult. It was difficult arriving there for starters. The new girl.

Mum brought me up to the gate, but Stephen wasn't there, and she didn't know the man who was there.

'Hello,' she said to the man. 'Is Stephen around?'

'No,' said the man, a little abruptly. 'I'm Patrick.'

'Okay,' said Mum, 'Hi, Patrick.'

'I'm the assistant manager,' Patrick said, again a little bluntly. As if Mum doubted that he was the assistant manager. Which I'm sure she didn't. He looked like an assistant manager. Tracksuit and everything.

'Well, this is Anna,' Mum said a little uncertainly. 'Stephen said that she could come down and train with you. The under-14s?'

'Okay,' said Patrick. 'The girls are over there.'

Not a 'welcome Anna', or 'how are you?', or 'what position do you play?' or even 'what's your second name?' I just said, 'Bye, Mum', and I walked over towards where the other girls were.

That was daunting: walking over to a group of girls who were talking and laughing. And just standing there, sort of beside them, sort of behind them, not really a part of it.

It was so different to Mountbridge. In Mountbridge, I was a part of it all right. I was a big part of it. I was at ease there, I was at home. I loved training in Mountbridge, with Sally and Evelyn and Kate and Hannah and everyone. I knew everyone there. I was comfortable and I loved that.

This was very different. I was the new girl. Nobody knew me and I knew nobody. Nobody spoke to me and I certainly wasn't going to speak to anyone before they spoke to me. I just stood there, looking down at the ground, looking at my feet, about a yard away from the other girls, and I started humming. 'Hard Day's Night'. I don't even particularly like that song, but I

41

started to hum it, just to take my mind off the fact that I was on my own. After what seemed like an eternity, Patrick came over.

'Okay girls, line up,' he said. 'You know the drill.'

I didn't know the drill, and Patrick surely knew that I didn't know the drill. The girls lined up, two behind two, and started jogging. I went towards the back of the line. I quickly did a count in twos, there was an even number of girls, fourteen or sixteen or eighteen. That was good. Meant that I wouldn't be on my own, the odd one out.

I let the girls jog ahead and I fell into line at the back of the group. But the girl who was left with me jogged along beside the two girls who were immediately in front of me, chatting as she jogged, so that the second last 'pair' was a 'pair' of three, and the last 'pair' was a 'pair' of one. Me!

Still nobody had spoken to me. It was as if I didn't exist.

'One!' shouted Patrick, and there was a collective stooping in front of me for a stride or two. I was the only one who remained upright.

'One!' shouted Patrick again, and all the girls stooped forward again as they jogged. It seemed like they were putting their left hands on the ground. I stooped forward a bit, half-heartedly.

'Two!' shouted Patrick, and the girls all stooped forward again. It appeared that they were touching the ground with their right hands this time, so I stooped forward and put my right hand on the ground.

'Four!' shouted Patrick, and all the girls jumped in the air, arms up, as if they were catching an imaginary ball. So I jumped too, about a half a second after the others.

'Five!' shouted Patrick, and the girl who was supposed to be jogging alongside me sprinted from the back of the line towards the front.

'Sprint!' shouted Patrick, looking at me. I just looked back at him, unsure of what to do, not certain if he was shouting at me directly or not. 'New girl!' he shouted. 'Sprint!'

That was unequivocal. (That means that I was in no doubt about what he meant. I learned that word when I was in sixth class, when Miss Ferguson said it in class one day and Sally asked her what it meant. Sally was being a bit cheeky, but Miss Ferguson explained it, and I remembered it. Strange how you get to know and remember things sometimes.)

So I took off. Ran as fast as I could from the back of the line and fell into step at the front beside the girl who had sprinted ahead of me.

At least somebody recognised my presence. 'New girl'. At least I knew that I wasn't a ghost.

The training itself was tough. Or the sprints were tough. The shuttles were grand, I was at least as fast as all of the girls and I was faster than most. But we did the shuttles for ages, and we did these 60-yard sprints at the end. They were the toughest. Six or seven in a row, flat out, with just a twenty-second rest in between sprints. And there was no hiding place, with Patrick screaming at you.

I gave everything, I was afraid not to, I was afraid of Patrick, but I felt a bit nauseous at the end of the third last one. At the end of the second last one, I puked. I actually got sick. Vomited. That had never happened to me in training before.

'New girl,' Patrick said. 'Are you okay there?'

'Yes,' I said. 'I'm fine.'

I didn't have the energy to say my name is Anna.

'Right come on,' he said to everyone. 'Last one. Give it everything you have.'

He made me do the last sprint too.

Finally, Patrick got the footballs out. I felt weak from the sprints, but it was good to get to play football. I felt comfortable when we were playing. I enjoyed the football drills. I enjoyed the foot passing and I enjoyed the shooting and I enjoyed the game at the end.

That's the thing about football: it rises above the cliques. When you are actually playing, when you are on the pitch, it doesn't matter who hangs out with whom off the pitch, or who is the coolest, or who has the nicest clothes, or who always has her homework done. All that matters is what's going on on the pitch. If you can play, when you are on the pitch you fit in.

I did fairly well in that first training session. I got plenty of the ball in the game at the end, I gave some nice passes and I scored two points.

This girl called Tina was dominant. She dominated the play and she dominated the talk. She looked for the ball all the time, even if she wasn't in the best position, and she gave out to the other girls very quickly. Often unfairly.

Another girl was very good, but she was quiet. She didn't say much, but she was a very good player. Debbie, they were calling her.

'Well done,' she said to me at the end of the game as we walked towards the gate.

'Thanks,' I said. 'Debbie, isn't it?'

'Yeah,' she said. 'Debbie, Debs, Deborah, Deb. People call me all sorts of things!'

We laughed.

'I'm Anna,' I said.

'You've just joined?'

'Yeah,' I said. 'We've moved from Galway. My mum grew up here.'

'Great,' said Debbie with a warm smile. 'How are you coping with everything? Big change for you, I'm sure.'

Before I could answer, a voice called from behind us.

'Hey Debs.' It was Tina. 'Is this your top?'

'Oh,' said Debbie as she put her hand to her head. 'Sorry. It is Tina. Thanks very much. I'd forget my head.'

Debbie ran back to where Tina was with her top. I didn't know what to do. Wait for Debbie, who was being nice, who was talking to me, the only person who had really spoken to me for the last hour and a half, or walk on towards the gate alone? I had to walk on. To do anything else would have come across as being too needy. Why did Tina have to call Debbie back? And why did Debbie have to forget her stupid top?

Then I saw Mum. She was standing at the gate, talking to a man in a dark green tracksuit. He had dark hair, quite slim, quite tall, stubbly face. Mum saw me as I approached and she smiled.

'And this is Anna,' she said to the man. 'My darling daughter.'

'Hi Anna,' said the man warmly as he extended his hand. 'I'm Stephen.'

I shook his hand. Stephen the manager. The man Mum had said she knew.

'How was training?' he asked me. 'Your first training session with Ballymarra?'

'It was fine,' I said politely.

'Were the girls nice to you?'

'They were,' I lied. 'I found the sprints a bit tough, but I enjoyed the ball work.'

'Ah yes,' said Stephen. 'Patrick does like to run the girls' lungs out.'

He laughed at Mum.

'Did he do his famous 60-yard sprints?'

'He did,' I said. A little embarrassed. I could still taste the remnants of sick in my mouth.

'Yeah,' said a voice from behind me. 'Anna struggled with the sprints. They mustn't be very fit in Galway.'

Tina was standing beside me, big grin on her face, before I could fully process what she had said.

'Hi, Tina,' said Stephen.

'Hi, Dad,' said Tina.

At least she knows my name, I thought.

'Can you take my gear home?' she said to Stephen, without breaking stride. 'I'm going with Mum.'

And she was gone. It was Stephen's turn to look a little embarrassed.

'That's my daughter,' he said to Mum.

'She seems nice,' said Mum.

'She's a good player,' I said.

'Hmm,' said Stephen. 'She needs to realise that she has teammates. She needs to pass more.'

And not give out to people as much as she does, I thought, but didn't say.

'There's no training on Wednesday,' said Stephen. 'There's a managers' meeting. But we have the championship on Sunday, the last game in the Round Robin. It's here, against Castleherron. You're okay for that Anna?'

I nodded. Dreading it already.

'Great,' he said. 'And it's great to see you again, Emma,' he said to Mum, as he gave her a kiss on the cheek. 'Maybe we'll see you on Sunday too?'

Now it was Mum's turn to look a little embarrassed.

'Maybe,' she said.

• • • • •

Chapter 7

NERVOUS

always felt nervous on the morning of a match. Even if the match was of little consequence, even if it was a challenge match. Even if I knew that I was playing well, if I was really confident in myself. And even if I knew that I wasn't going to start. I just felt nervous on match day. Always.

So I was nervous that Sunday morning. I woke up nervous. I was nervous when I was looking for my gear and I was nervous when I was eating my porridge at the kitchen table.

'Are you nervous?' asked Grandad.

'No,' I said.

Mum was standing behind me at the fridge, getting the orange juice out. She stroked my head.

'She's always a little nervous on match day,' she said. 'Aren't you pet?'

I dug my spoon into my porridge.

'Not always,' I protested. 'And I won't even be starting today.'

'You don't know that,' said Mum. 'You thought you did well in training on Monday? Right?'

'Mum!' I said, exasperated. 'They're not going to start me. The new girl. If Cora Staunton moved into Ballymarra, they wouldn't start her. They couldn't. It wouldn't be fair on all the other girls.'

'But you'll probably come on,' said Mum. 'At some stage.'

'Maybe,' I said. 'But maybe not. I've only had one training session.'

In the back of my mind, I desperately wanted to start. I always wanted to start. Even when I played for the Under-16s in Mountbridge with the older girls, even when I was the youngest player on the panel. I was small, but I always wanted to start. I used to see who was there and who was missing. If one of the six forwards was away or injured, there was always a good chance that I would start.

I knew that it was unlikely though. I thought that I was worth my place on the team for sure, probably on the half-forward line, maybe even centre half-forward. But, like I said to Mum, they really couldn't start me. It wouldn't have been fair. It wouldn't have been right.

'Your new gear is in the car,' said Mum. 'In the boot.'

I opened the front door, went out to the car and opened the boot. There was my gear: black shorts, green socks, both wrapped in cellophane. I picked up the two packages and crinkled the wrapping. I loved the crinkly sound that the cellophane made.

'Got them!'

I unwrapped the shorts in the kitchen and put them on. They fitted nicely. Then I unwrapped the socks.

'When did you pick up the socks and the shorts?' I asked Mum.

'Stephen gave them to me on Tuesday evening,' she said.

'Monday evening,' I said.

'What?'

'Monday evening,' I said again. 'There was no training on Tuesday evening. You saw Stephen on Monday evening.'

Mum took a sip of her tea. Or her coffee. You could never tell with Mum.

'Eh, no,' she said. 'It was Tuesday evening. I saw Stephen on Tuesday evening as well.'

Grandad stood up and took his bowl over to the sink.

'He dropped the gear in,' he said. 'Didn't he, Em?'

'He did,' said Mum.

'Well then what was it doing in your car?' I asked.

'What?'

'Why was the gear in your car? If he dropped it in?'

To be honest, I didn't really care why the gear was in Mum's car. I just thought it was odd. And the whole conversation was just starting to get irritating now.

'I don't really know,' said Mum, looking at Grandad. 'I must have been outside. I must have been going somewhere just after he dropped it in.'

'Out to see Denise?'

'Sorry pet?'

'To see Denise. You went out with Denise on Tuesday evening.'

'Yes!' said Mum, as if she had just figured out the answer to some complex mathematical problem. 'Out to see Denise,' she said. Delighted with herself. 'I was out with Denise on Tuesday. I must have been just about to get into the car and go to see her when Stephen dropped in the gear.'

Grandad sighed and turned on the tap.

☣ ☣ ☣

I was nervous going into the dressing room. Mum couldn't come with me, of course. I had to brave this alone. This was like the first day of training, but different.

In a way, it was easier. For starters, I wasn't the brand new girl any more. I was still the new girl, but at least I had met them at training. Only one training session, but it was something. I had got to know the girls a little bit. And I had played well in that training session. They would have seen that I could play a bit. That had to count for something.

As well as that, match day is very different to training day. Everyone is relaxed at training, joking and laughing, catching up. Even wearing their own gear. On match day, people are more focused. Managers as well as players. Things are more formal, more serious. There is something at stake.

Stephen and Patrick were standing outside the dressing room door.

'Hi, Anna,' said Stephen.

'Hi, Stephen,' I said, more quietly than I had intended. 'Hi, Patrick.'

Better. Patrick nodded.

'Get in there and get yourself ready,' Stephen said as I opened the door.

Most of the girls were there already. There was a bit of a space between two of the girls at the far side of the dressing room, between Debbie and Aoife, so I made my way over there and sat down.

'Hi,' said Debbie quietly.

There was a quiet hum around the dressing room. Girls were talking to each other, but quietly in twos and threes. There was a nervousness about the place. I didn't say much to anyone. I just quietly put on my black shorts and my green socks and my boots.

Suddenly the door burst open, and Tina and Sinéad walked in.

'Right, girls,' shouted Tina. Quiet hum over. 'This is it. The championship. Last game in the Round Robin. Lose this, and we're out. Lose it and we only have the league for the rest of the season. Win it, and we're into the quarter-final. The chance of going all the way. And it's Castleherron, for God's sake. We never lose to Castleherron. And we're not going to start today.'

Uncertain silence.

'Are we?'

A few mumbles. No, we're not.

'Well, are we?'

A few more mumbles. A little more loudly. 'No, we're not.'

'ARE WE???'

'NO WE ARE NOT!!!'

There was a knock on the door.

'Everybody decent?' called Stephen.

'YES!' came the chorus.

Stephen and Patrick and one of the mums came in, and stood behind the pile of jerseys. Stephen peeled the orange jersey off the top of the pile and threw it to Sofia, calling her name as he threw it. Sofia allowed the jersey land on her head, so that it covered her whole head and face and shoulders. Everybody laughed. Goal-keepers!

'Rebecca, you're right corner-back,' said Stephen as he threw one of the green shirts to her. Number two. Rebecca caught the jersey and quickly put it on over her under armour.

'Robyn, full-back,' as he threw number three to her.

'Edel, left corner-back.'

Number four.

Stephen continued to call the girls' names as he threw the jerseys out.

Sandra number five, right half-back. Shauna, number

six, centre-half. Orla number 7, left-half. Lily, number 8, centre field. Tina, number 9, also centre field. Debbie, number 10, Sinéad, number 11, Shelley, number 12.

I hoped that I would sneak on in the corner. Number 15 maybe, left corner-forward.

'And number 15,' said Stephen. He looked around the room. I thought that his gaze fell on me for a second and my heart leapt. Was I starting?

'Aoife,' he said, as he threw the jersey to Aoife beside me.

'And subs,' he said. 'Stay warm and dry,' as he threw a jersey to me.

Number 17.

'That rain is wet and it's unusually cold. Most of you will be getting a run at some stage.'

We filed out, one by one. A few of the girls were shouting. 'Come on Ballymarra! Come on girls!' But most were quiet. I was quiet. I was never really a shouter, not even in Mountbridge, not even when I knew everybody well.

I glanced at the goals, behind the goals, but there was nobody there. I didn't expect to see anyone. Not any more. No chats, no pre-match ritual. No Daddy. I didn't cry.

We did some stretches, and we did a hand-passing drill, just to warm up. Then a foot-passing drill. I had a look at the Castleherron girls down at the other goals. They were just all lining up and kicking balls in towards the goals. They didn't seem to have any structured warm-up.

Stephen called us all in and we huddled together just as the rain got heavier. He went over everybody's role. Sofia, careful with your kick-outs. Give the short one if it's on, but if it isn't, look for Tina or Lily in the middle of the field. Defenders, stay tight. Half-backs, don't be afraid to go forward if it's on. Forwards, be sure to pass if someone else is in a better position. Debbie, don't be afraid to shoot.

Subs, stay warm and dry. I got it.

I went back to the dressing room to get my coat. All our other subs were in club track suits, but I didn't have one and, even if I had had one, I still would have got my coat. I was annoyed that I wasn't starting. I understood it. I was new. But I was still annoyed. But I understood it.

But I was still annoyed.

Strange thing about being a sub. You want your team to do well, you want your team to win, but you also want someone to play badly so that you will get on. Or get injured. But you never really hope that one of your teammates gets injured. Not badly injured anyway. And if you do, you never admit it to anyone. You don't even admit it to yourself.

Aoife didn't have a good first half. She kicked one wide and she gave the ball away twice. Tina shouted at her both times. Ah Aoife! Maybe Stephen would put me on for Aoife at half-time.

He didn't. Everyone was doing well, according to his half-time talk. We were two points ahead, and we deserved to be further ahead. He was right. We were the better team by a fair way.

You could see the good players too. It quickly becomes apparent who the stronger players are.

Sinéad was good and Robyn was good and Lily was good. And Sofia was a good goalkeeper, even if her kick-outs were a little weak. Edel was weak enough, and Aoife wasn't having a great game, and Rebecca tried hard, but she struggled against the Castleherron number 15.

Debbie was good, but she was quiet. She was skilful, she could kick a score, she could pick out a pass and, while she was left-footed, she could kick with both feet. But she probably lacked a little bit of confidence. She passed the ball when she was in a position to shoot, sometimes even when she was in a better position than the girl to whom she passed.

The more the second half went on, the less willing I was to go on. I was getting wetter and I was getting colder. The last thing I wanted to do was take off my coat. Then Tina kicked that free over the bar, four points up, and Stephen called me. My opportunity. My five minutes. And I messed it up.

Even though we won, I didn't feel good. I hadn't touched the ball. I didn't really feel like I was a part of it. All the girls were congratulating each other, one or two even said well done to me. I just smiled. I was soaking wet and I hadn't contributed anything.

On the bright side, we had won. We were into the quarter-final. I hoped that I would get another opportunity.

Chapter 8

FIRST DAY

I used to like Monday mornings. I used to like going back to school to see my friends, hear what they did for the weekend, and catch up on everything. And I always liked school. I always liked Maths and English and Irish and History.

That was primary school though.

Maybe I would have continued to like Monday mornings if we had stayed in Galway and I had gone to secondary school there, to St Vincent's, with Sally and Kate and Evelyn and Hannah.

The last Monday in August was awful. My first day back at school. My first at school in Ballymarra. My first in secondary school.

It was first years only that day. Give the first years a day, give them a chance to get used to the new school before you bring the second years and the third years and all the other years in on top of them.

Mum drove me to school that day, and she walked me to the gate. I wanted her to come in with me. I wanted her to walk through the gate with me, to walk up to the school doors with me, to walk in through the front door with me, to walk to my classroom with me, to make sure that I was in the right classroom, to sit in the desk beside me, to stay there all day. Or to take me back home with her. But, at the same time, I didn't want her to walk in with me at all.

None of the other mums or dads were going into the school grounds. Very few were even going up to the gate. Some kids were getting out of cars, others were walking up to the gate in groups.

'Okay, Mum,' I said. 'You'd better go now.'

She grabbed me and hugged me. I hesitated at first, well aware of how this would look to the other kids. Hugging Mummy at the school gate. But then I could feel the tears coming, and I buried my head in her shoulder. I stayed there until I thought that I had the tears under control.

'You'll be great,' Mum said. 'You're brilliant. Just be yourself.'

The whole day was a struggle. I didn't know anybody. I saw one or two of the girls from football, but they looked different in their school uniforms and with their hair down, I wasn't sure who was who and I wasn't sure of their names, and they didn't really talk to me anyway. They stayed in their own groups.

I tried to console myself with the thought that everybody else was in the same boat as me. All first years. All new to secondary school. But, actually, nobody was in the same boat as me as far as I could tell. Everybody else seemed to know everybody else, or somebody else at least.

I sat on a bench in the yard at break time and watched all the other girls playing and chatting. All in groups or in pairs. I had lunch on my own in the canteen, at a table on my own. A ham and cheese sandwich, a yogurt drink, an apple and a Time Out bar, with a flask of tea.

'Is that a flask of tea?' some giggly girl asked from the table beside me.

'It is,' I said.

She turned to her friend and laughed.

I held it together until the evening. I walked home on my own, got to Granny and Grandad's front door, opened the door with my new key, took my shoes off, climbed the stairs in my socks, got into my bedroom and flung my orange schoolbag onto the floor. Then I flung myself onto my bed, and I bawled my eyes out.

Mum and Granny and Grandad were great that evening. They made such a fuss of me. And I called Sally. She made me laugh and she made it sound like her first day at St Vincent's in Galway was as bad as my first day at St Raphael's in Ballymarra. I'm sure that it wasn't. She had Evelyn and Hannah and Kate. But it was nice of Sally to make it sound like it was.

I expected Tuesday to be worse than Monday, but it wasn't. It was actually better. I was surprised. On Tuesday, the whole school was back, all the second years, all the sixth years. I thought that the bigger crowds would make it even more daunting for me, but it didn't. Quite the opposite actually. I suppose the fact that I was on my own was more noticeable when there were fewer people there. To me as well as to everyone else.

And a girl was nice to me at lunch. She wasn't over-the-top nice, she was just normal nice. She was sitting at the next table over from me with her friends. Probably second years, I thought.

I recognised her from the football team. Orla. Orla Cambridge. She played in the half-back line, and she was good. She was small, but she was tough.

She told me that she knew how difficult it was, being in first year, being on your own. That it would only get better.

She said that it couldn't get any worse anyway! That made me laugh.

It's amazing how one act of just-a-little-kindness from one person can completely lift another person's day. Orla Cambridge lifted my day that day, my second day at school, higher than she ever could have imagined.

Chapter 9

• • • • •

NO SOCKS

'**W**here are my socks, Mum?' I shouted, as I dug deep into my football socks and shorts drawer.

'They're in your sock drawer,' Mum called back. Sounded like she was downstairs. 'Where else would socks be?'

'No,' I shouted. 'My football socks.'

Silence.

'Mum?'

'Ehhhh,' said Mum, a little more quietly. 'If they're not in your football socks and shorts drawer, then they're still in the wash.'

Bah. I closed the drawer and walked out of my room to the top of the stairs.

'I don't need to have my green socks,' I shouted from the top of the stairs. 'It's only a challenge match. My navy socks or my black socks should be grand.'

Again, silence.

'Mum?'

'Yes, pet. Also in the wash.'

'Both pairs?'

'Yes, pet, both pairs.'

'Ah, Mum.'

'Stop shouting at me from upstairs,' Mum shouted back. 'Come down here if you want to have a conversation with me.'

Charlie came out of his room with his hands over his ears.

'Yeah, Anna,' he said. 'Stop shouting!'

I went back into my room. This is what happens when you only have three pairs of football socks. It wasn't enough. Not when your mother only does the laundry when the clothes spill out over the top of the laundry basket and into the bathroom and practically down the stairs. And we'd had all the arguments about me doing my own laundry. I didn't agree that I was big enough and bold enough.

I opened my normal sock drawer and started to rummage around. Maybe there were socks in there that looked a little bit like football socks. It was only a challenge match. I was sure that I could get away with not having the club socks.

I heard a crinkling of plastic as I rummaged around. I dug deep into my socks, and there they were. The bright orange socks. Cellophane still around them. The ones that Daddy had given me that morning when he came into my room. The last time I saw him.

I just looked at them for a few seconds. Badly wrapped in cellophane that had been opened and closed a few times. It felt like being punched in the stomach: I felt weak, powerless, as if my heart had a mind of its own. My throat felt tight and dried up and my eyes felt stingy and welled up and, suddenly, there were tears streaming down my face. And I was sobbing. Visibly. Audibly. Uncontrollably. And before I knew what was happening, Mum had me in her arms and my face was buried in her shoulder.

After a few minutes, when I felt that I could speak, I pushed back from Mum's shoulder.

'They're the socks,' I sobbed.

'I know, pet.'

There were tears in Mum's eyes too.

'They're the socks that Daddy gave me.'

'I know,' Mum said as she gripped me even more tightly. 'I found them when we were moving.'

Mum pulled me close to her again, and we both had a good cry. Charlie came in and looked at us.

'You can shout if you want, Anna.'

Mum and I just laughed and grabbed him. We both kissed him continually as he struggled to get away from us. He succeeded. He escaped our clutches and bolted out of the room.

'Mum, I'm going to wear them,' I said.

'You don't have to, pet,' Mum said. 'I can wash your green socks and throw them into the tumble drier. They should be dry in an hour.'

'Nah, that's probably not soon enough, I have to leave in a half an hour. And anyway, I should wear the socks. Daddy bought them for me, for me to wear them. Not so that they could sit in the bottom of my sock drawer.'

'It's up to you, pet,' said Mum. 'I'm sure that he'd be very happy for you to wear them.'

I picked up the socks and carefully opened the cellophane. I took the socks out of their wrapper and placed them carefully in my gear bag, on top of my towel, beside my boots.

☣ ☣ ☣

There was a different atmosphere in the dressing room before this match. It was a match, but it was only a challenge. Against Croughton. Stephen had arranged it because the quarter-final had been delayed by two weeks. Just so that we could retain our match-sharpness, he had said.

It wouldn't be the end of the world if we lost. We wouldn't be out of the championship and we wouldn't lose points in the league. That said, we wanted to win. We all wanted to win. It was somewhere between a training session and a competitive match.

I opened my bag and took out my boots and put them on the dressing room floor in front of me. I took out my shorts and placed them carefully on the seat beside me. Then I took out my socks. My luminous orange socks.

I put on the left one first. I always put on my left sock first. I'm not superstitious. Honestly. Really I'm not. I just always put my left sock on first.

I pulled it up high, up to my knee, and I folded the top of the sock down, so that the top of the sock sat just beneath my knee. Some of the girls were wearing short socks, and some of the others were wearing long socks, but had them folded down so that they only came half way up their shins. I liked wearing long socks though, and I liked to wear them long, pulled up to my knee.

I put on the right sock, and did the same thing. I pulled it up high, up to my knee, then folded it down so that the top of my sock sat just below my knee. They fit perfectly. Tight, snug, comfortable. I thought of Daddy, but I didn't feel sad. I felt assured. Confident. As if he was sitting beside me in the dressing room.

And I was starting. Number 15, Stephen had said. Left full-forward. The last name on the team sheet.

To be honest, I was a little surprised that I was starting. I hadn't done anything to enhance my claims to a place in the starting line-up in Sunday's game. But I had done well in training, so maybe Stephen was going by that.

Aoife was first substitute, number 16. I'm not sure that she was too pleased about that.

I felt good as we left the dressing room and jogged towards the pitch. I felt as if I belonged. Not an outsider, not the new girl, but part of the team. Maybe it was because I had been selected to start. Maybe it was because of my new socks. But that was crazy. It couldn't have been because of my new socks.

I saw Mum on the sideline as I ran out onto the pitch. She was standing with some of the other mums and dads. She smiled and waved. I half-waved back. I didn't like interacting with people before or during matches. I wanted to concentrate. I wanted to focus only on the match.

It was different before. Daddy and I had a ritual. It wasn't something that we agreed or ever really spoke about, it was just something that developed between us. After I left the dressing room and ran out onto the pitch, I would always go over to Daddy. It would always be the first thing that I would do.

He would always be behind the goals that were closest to the dressing room, or, if the dressing room was in the centre of the pitch, to the left of the dressing room. Obviously, we didn't know before the match which way we were playing, so we didn't know into which goals we were shooting.

It didn't matter whether we were playing at home or playing away, and it didn't matter who else was at the match, even if Mum was at the match. He would be behind the goals closest to the dressing room, or to the left of the dressing room, on his own. Always. So that I would know where to find him.

I would run over to him and we would put our arms

71

on each other's shoulders and put our heads together.

'Are you ready?' he would say softly.

'I am,' I would say.

'Tuned in?' he would say.

'Tuned in,' I would say.

'So, concentrate on what is happening on the pitch,' he would say. 'For the next hour, that's all that matters. Focused on the pitch. Okay?'

'Okay,' I would say.

'Take responsibility,' he would say. 'Don't leave it to somebody else. Okay?'

'Okay,' I would say.

'And do your best,' he would say. 'That's all you can do. Okay?'

'Okay,' I would say.

Then he would put his hands on my head and he would kiss me on the forehead. That was it. Every time. All of that. Before every game. Then I would be off to warm up, fully motivated and fully focused, and bursting with energy and confidence.

These days, I just had to tune myself in. Concentrate on the game and the pitch.

I ran over to the dressing room goals and put my hands on the fence behind the goals, closed my eyes, and thought of Daddy.

Ready.

Tuned in.

Concentrate on what is happening on the pitch.

Focused on the pitch.

Take responsibility.

Do your best.

I felt good. As if he was there with me.

The game was intense from the start. Tina won the toss and chose to play into the road goals, the goals that were closest to the dressing room. The girls called the road goals the scoring goals, they thought that it was easier to score into those goals for some reason and, if there was no wind, Tina always chose to play into those goals in the first half if she won the toss.

Tina also won the throw-in and soloed forward. She soloed three or four times, which took her across the 45-metre line. I came off my marker from my starting position at left full-forward and called for the ball.

'Tina!'

Tina kicked the ball in my direction. It bounced in front of me, but I managed to jump and catch it at around nose level. I landed running and free. My marker was behind me somewhere.

I didn't care. I hopped the ball once and tapped it on my toe once and looked up at the goals. Tina was calling for the ball to my right, but I blocked her out of my mind. I was twenty-five yards out and I had a clear shot.

I hit the ball with the inside of my right foot. I aimed for the right-hand upright, aiming to draw the ball in and around and over the bar. It didn't look like it was curling in at first, but then it started to move in the air. I knew that I had the distance, I knew that the ball was going to reach the goals. It was just a case of accuracy then.

The ball curled around really nicely. It moved a little to the left, so that there was as much space between the ball and the left upright as there was between the ball and the right upright.

As the ball sailed over the bar, I had a surge of lots of emotions, all clambering for recognition. Elation and pride and ecstasy and delight all at the same time.

'Well done,' said Amanda.

'Great score,' said Debbie.

'Brilliant, Anna,' Stephen shouted from the sideline.

I jogged back to my position at left full-forward, bursting with pride, and I looked back at the goals, where the Croughton goalkeeper was getting ready to take the kick-out. Beyond the umpire, behind the goals, there seemed to be a shadow. It wasn't a sunny day, there shouldn't have been a shadow, but there seemed to be one there. It was in the shape of a man, slim build, quite tall.

I looked away for a second or two, then looked back at the goals. The shadow was still there, behind the umpire, just behind the goals. Its arms appeared to be above its head, and it appeared to be moving them forwards and backwards, almost imperceptibly. As if it was cheering, as if it was celebrating.

'No way,' I said out loud. 'Daddy?'

Chapter 10

WELL PLAYED

I played well in that game against Croughton. I played
very well. I scored five points and we won easily,
2-14 to 1-7.

Stephen moved me from left full-forward to left half-
forward at half-time, and he moved me to centre half-
forward with about fifteen minutes to go. I grew in
confidence as the game went on. I loved playing centre
half-forward, in the middle of the attack. I got loads
of the ball, I passed and I moved and I called for it. I
shot when the shot was on and I passed when the pass
was on. My shots were accurate and my passing was
sharp and my decision-making was good. I don't think

I made one bad decision in the entire match.

It was the first time that I had played well since Daddy died. It was the first time that I came off the pitch, knowing that I did as well as I could have done. I felt great. I felt fulfilled.

The shadow stayed behind the road goals for the entire first half but – strange thing – I couldn't see it when I was close to it. It was only when I was far away. Like a mist or a fog that you can't see when you are in it. It was always blurry, always ill-defined, so that I wasn't sure if it was really there or not.

I went down to the road goals at half-time. I walked around behind the goals, but there was nothing there. Then, bizarrely, for the second half, there appeared to be a shadow behind the river goals, the goals into which we were shooting in the second half.

I wasn't put off by the shadow. Or what I thought was a shadow. On the contrary, I was assured by it. Strangely, even though it was on my mind, it didn't seem to affect my concentration on the match. I was thinking about the shadow, but at the same time I was thinking clearly about the game. My positioning, where I wanted to be on the pitch, what I wanted to do with the ball when I got it.

Perhaps Croughton weren't very good. It seemed

that I always had space to pass or to shoot or to move. I was first to every ball, I won nearly every ball that I contested. It was just one of those rare games in which just about everything seemed to go right.

It was only a challenge match, it didn't really matter on lots of levels, but it's always good to win, and it mattered to me. I was walking on air as I walked off the pitch. All the girls were saying 'well done' to me. Edel said 'well done'. Debbie told me that I played great. Even Aoife.

Aoife had come on as a sub with fifteen minutes to go. Stephen took Sinéad off to move me to centre half-forward and he put Aoife on left half-forward. Aoife kicked a good point too. I just said 'well done' to her as well.

I saw Mum as I got to the sideline. She was beaming. Her smile went from the bottom of her left ear to the bottom of her right ear. It looked like there were tears in her eyes, although maybe it was just the wind. She grabbed me as I got to her.

'Mum!' I protested. 'I'm all sweaty!'

'I don't care,' said Mum.

I stood there for a second or two, the warmth of her chest against my face.

'You were brilliant pet,' she said. 'Just brilliant.'

I took my face away and looked into her eyes. The water had escaped from her left eye and was making its way in a tiny stream down her cheek.

'Thanks, Mum,' I said. She rubbed her cheek with her fingers. 'Are you okay?' I asked.

'I haven't been as okay in a long time,' she said. 'Now, go and get your stuff. I'll wait in the car.'

The smile was imprinted on my face as I left her and started walking towards the dressing room.

Stephen was walking towards me, beaming.

'Well done, Anna,' he said. 'You were great.'

I just smiled continued to walk towards the dressing room. Sinéad and Tina were just behind me.

'Hey, Anna,' Tina called.

I turned around and stopped.

'You should have passed that last one to me,' she said.

'What?'

'That last ball,' said Tina. 'You should have passed to me.'

'What last ball?' I asked. I genuinely didn't know which ball she was talking about. 'The one I kicked over the bar?'

'Yes,' said Tina. 'That one.'

'But I scored,' I said. 'I kicked it over the bar.'

'Yes,' said Tina. 'But I could have scored a goal.'

I thought she was joking. I was sure she was joking. But she wasn't smiling. She wasn't joking.

'Tina, seriously,' I said. 'You were out to the side. And there were at least three players between you and the goal, and the goalkeeper. It is unlikely that you would have scored a goal. And I was in a much better position to take a point than you were. I thought about passing to you, but I decided that the best option was to shoot. The point was there for the taking, so I took it.'

'There weren't three players between me and the goal,' she said. 'I was in on goal. I only had the goal-keeper to beat.'

Sinéad wasn't saying anything. She was just walking along with us, looking a bit sheepish. Sinéad always looked a bit sheepish, which made sense. Sinéad was a bit of a sheep.

'You weren't in on goal, Tina,' I said.

'I was.'

'Ah Tina, for God's sake,' I said. 'Get over yourself.'

The words were out before I could stop myself. I had never before told someone to get over themselves, and I hadn't heard anyone tell Tina to get over herself. In fact, I hadn't seen anyone stand up to Tina yet. It appeared that people just nodded when Tina spoke and agreed. Even her best friends. Even her dad.

'What did you say to me?'

Tina grabbed my right arm. I stopped walking and she stopped beside me. She looked me squarely in the eye, threateningly. I returned her glare. She still had a hold of my arm, but I didn't flinch. It was important not to flinch. I was surprised at how at ease I was with this. I wasn't normally this comfortable with confrontation.

I could feel the nail of Tina's thumb digging into my bicep. I could feel it hurt, but I didn't care. It didn't really hurt, I didn't really feel the pain. In a strange way, I was enjoying the adrenaline rush.

I couldn't back down. I chose my tone carefully. I spoke deliberately and distinctly.

'I said,' I said slowly, 'get over yourself.'

I could feel Tina's thumbnail dig more deeply into my muscle. Her face started to cloud over with rage, and I dared her with my eyes to push me further. It looked like she was on the brink of eruption, and I was comfortable with that. I just stood there, at ease with the increasing pain in my right arm, comfortable with whatever was going to happen next.

'Girls!' shouted Stephen from behind us. 'What's going on?'

The rage-cloud on Tina's face started to clear. You

could see it happen. Noticeably. Visibly. It was a process and it happened quickly. Like a time-lapse of a stormy day turning into a clear day.

'Nothing, Dad,' said Tina.

She relaxed her grip on my arm.

'I was just telling Anna how well she played.'

Chapter 11

• • • • • •

TINA ISN'T HAPPY

I t was nice to get home.

'Well?' asked Granny. 'How did you do?'

'We won,' I said.

'That's great,' said Granny. 'And were you on?'

'I was.'

'Did you start?'

'I did.'

'Great. And how did you play?'

'I played okay.'

Granny smiled.

'She didn't play okay,' said Mum quietly. 'She played great. She was brilliant.'

'Oh that's great,' said Granny. 'Fantastic.'

I smiled.

'Do you think she deserves a cup of hot chocolate, Ems?'

Mum looked at me and smiled.

'I think she deserves a bucket of hot chocolate Granny!'

Mum called Granny 'Granny' when she spoke to her for Charlie or me. She called her 'Mum' though when she was talking to her about grown-up stuff. I always thought that it sounded strange when Mum called Granny Mum.

I took off my boots in the utility room and hung them up on the hooks on the back of the utility room door. I ran upstairs, took off my shorts and put them into the laundry basket. My gear was all sweaty, but I was happy. I could feel the smile on my face. Then I took off my t-shirt and put it into the laundry basket. Then I took off my socks.

I didn't put my socks, my bright orange socks, straight into the laundry basket. I just held them there in my hands and looked at them. They were wet and they were sweaty, but they looked great.

Could there be something about the socks? A link to Daddy? Crazy thought. It was ridiculous to even think that.

I remembered Daddy's words. *They will make you play the best football that you have ever played in your entire life.* I know. Crazy.

I put the socks into the laundry basket and closed the lid. Then I put on my dressing gown and went back down to the kitchen where Granny was waiting with my steaming cup of hot chocolate.

☣ ☣ ☣

It rained on Monday morning. There were lots of cars trying to get into the school car park, so I just got out of Mum's car at the gate and walked in from there.

There were a few people in my classroom when I got there. Not many. About six or seven. I was early. I put my bag on the floor and turned sleepily to hang up my coat.

'Well played yesterday,' said a voice behind me.

I turned to see Robyn and Rebecca. They both looked so different in their school uniforms. On the pitch, togged out, hair tied back, they were athletic and sporty. In school though, in school uniforms, they looked like schoolgirls.

Robyn had her hair down, long dark brown hair, the front tied back with a bobbin, not dissimilar to the way that I had my hair. Rebecca had her blonde hair in a ponytail, but she looked different in her glasses.

'Thanks,' I said.

I wasn't sure which of them had said 'well played'.

'It was a good win wasn't it? Like, we all played well.'

'It was,' said Robyn. 'It was only a challenge match, you know, but it was good to win it. It's always good to beat Croughton. They're meanies. My dad works with one of their selectors, and he's always on about football. My dad says that you can't shut him up on the Monday after a match if they have won. He said that he was going to take a sick day if they had beaten us yesterday!'

We all laughed.

'Well played yourself, Robyn,' I said. 'And you, Rebecca. You look different in glasses!'

'Yeah, I'm blind as a bat if I don't wear glasses or contact lenses. My mum says I'm blind even when I do wear glasses.'

'It's not easy for you Anna, is it?' said Robyn. I looked at her. I didn't know what she meant. That Daddy had died? Did she know that Daddy had died? That I was new to the school? 'You know, coming to a new place,' Robyn continued hesitantly. 'Trying to break into a new team. Like, trying to get to know all of us. Trying to fit in.'

I wasn't sure, but I thought that she was being nice.

'I can imagine that that's hard,' she said. 'And a new school.'

'It's okay,' I lied.

'And you stood up to Tina!' Rebecca blurted.

Robyn gave her a thump on the arm and glared at her.

'I know!' said Rebecca. 'I'm sorry!'

I was confused.

'I know that I wasn't supposed to say anything,' said Rebecca.

'Three minutes,' Robyn said, disappointment in her voice. 'We haven't been talking to Anna for three minutes, and already you've brought it up.'

Rebecca just looked at Robyn apologetically. Wide-mouthed, somewhere between a grimace and a grin.

'What's going on?' I asked quietly.

'It's all the talk,' said Rebecca.

Robyn glowered.

'What's all the talk?' I asked.

'You and Tina,' said Rebecca.

'What?!'

'You and Tina,' said Rebecca again.

'Me and Tina what?'

Rebecca just looked at Robyn. She looked like she

was going to burst. She looked like she wanted Robyn to release the valve, relieve the pressure.

'Look, it's not all the talk really,' said Robyn slowly. 'But it has been mentioned. Did you and Tina have some kind of a fight after the match?'

'No,' I said.

'Really?' asked Robyn.

'Well, she told me that she thought that I should have passed to her there in the second half,' I said. 'She said that she thought she could have scored a goal. I told her that I didn't think I should have passed. That was it.'

'That was it?' asked Rebecca.

'That was it,' I said simply.

'Did she not grab your arm?'

'She did grab my arm actually,' I said.

'And what did you do?'

'I just looked at her.'

'And?'

'And nothing,' I said. 'Stephen came along. We went in to the dressing room, got our stuff and then I went home and had a hot chocolate.'

'That's not what they're saying,' said Rebecca.

'What are they saying?' I asked. 'And who are they?!'

'They're saying that you stood up to Tina,' said Rebecca.

'Really?' I asked. 'I didn't really. Honestly. They must have very little to be talking about. Whoever they are.'

'Nobody ever stands up to Tina,' said Robyn. 'What Tina says goes. That's just the way it is. It was like that in primary school, it's like that now in secondary school. It's like that on the football team.'

'I didn't know that,' I said. 'I know she's captain and all, and that she talks a lot. That's all. And I knew that she was in second year. But Debbie's in second year. Lily's in second year. They don't go pushing people around. Edel and Sinéad are in second year. And I just didn't think that Tina was right in this case, so I told her that. I told her what I thought. That's all.'

'It's not all,' said Rebecca. 'Tina isn't happy. She isn't happy that people are talking about it. They're saying that she wants to fight you.'

'Who are they?!'

The door opened suddenly and Lily ran in.

'Tina's on her way!' she exclaimed.

Before I could fully process that piece of information, Tina was standing in front of me, Sinéad beside her on her right, Edel beside her on her left.

Tina saw me as soon as she came into the room. She walked over to me and stood close. I just stood there.

'You and me. Patterson's Lane. After school today.'

This was scary. Tina was scary. I wasn't in the school very long, but I knew that Patterson's Lane was where you went when you wanted to fight somebody. I didn't want to fight somebody. I didn't want to fight Tina. I didn't want to fight anybody.

'Okay?'

Tina looked fearsome.

'No, not okay,' I managed to mutter.

'What's that?' asked Tina fiercely.

'I can't hear you. All I can hear is a little mouse squeak.'

'Not okay,' I said again.

I tried to say it more loudly, but I didn't really succeed.

This was petrifying.

'Are you afraid?' Tina mocked, as she looked around at Sinéad and Edel, who were both smiling nervously.

'I don't want to fight you Tina,' I protested.

'Are you scared?' asked Tina.

It was rhetorical. I was sure of it. She didn't give me a chance to answer anyway. She took a step towards me and pushed me back. It wasn't a hard push, but it took me aback. I winced with surprise and I took a step back. My legs felt weak. I was shocked. I felt threatened. I couldn't speak, and I wouldn't have known what to say even if I could have spoken.

A crowd started to gather. I couldn't see faces. I was transfixed on Tina's face. The other faces were just blurred visions, background noise. There was a rumble from the assembled girls. No shouts, no cheers, just a rumble of I didn't really know what. Anticipation. Discomfort. Excitement. Uncertainty.

I felt like crying. I wanted to burst into tears. I wasn't in pain. Tina's push wasn't painful. It was the suddenness of it. The intimidating nature of it. It was also the attention, the focus on me, the embarrassment. I fought hard against the tears. Don't cry now. Whatever you do, don't cry.

How did I get here? In front of this girl, this situation, full of menace, filled with malice, and a crowd around us? All I wanted was to fit in. Keep my head down. Play football and get along with some of the girls. Get on with the teachers. Get on with school. Keep a low profile. The last thing I wanted was attention.

'Come on, Tina.'

I recognised that voice. It was soft and warm and friendly.

'Leave her alone. I think she's learned her lesson.'

I couldn't see the girl's face, I couldn't release myself from Tina's gaze. It was another one of the blurred masses, but I knew that it was Debbie's voice. The jaw muscles in Tina's face started to relax, but there was still an anger in her eyes. She looked at me sternly.

'Have you?'

There was a steeliness in her voice.

'Have you learned your lesson?'

I nodded.

'Come on, Tina,' said Debbie. 'Farrell will be along in a minute. You don't want to be up in her office again.'

Tina reached out her right hand and moved it slowly towards me. I didn't know what she was going to do, but I felt defenceless against whatever it was going to be. She could have punched me in the face and I wouldn't have been able to do anything to protect myself. It was a weird feeling. Helplessness. Powerlessness.

Tina rested her right hand on my left cheek. She patted my cheek. Once, twice, three times. I just stood there, passively. The pats weren't strong enough to be slaps, but they were strong enough to be noticeable.

'Nah, you're right, Debs,' Tina said. 'She's not worth it.'

They left. Tina and Sinéad and Edel. The second years. Debbie left too, but she looked back at me as she left. I was very grateful to her. The crowd started to disperse. Some left the room, some went to the coat racks, and some went to their desks and sat down. Drama over.

I turned around slowly to face the coat racks. I put my left hand up to my left cheek. My cheek felt a little warm. I bent down to pick up my schoolbag, which was still on the floor beside me.

'Are you okay?'

I looked up to see Robyn there, with Rebecca beside her. They both looked concerned.

I nodded.

'Yeah.'

I was still fighting back the tears.

'Don't mind Tina,' said Robyn as she put her hand gently on my shoulder.

'She's just a big bully.'

• • • • • •

Chapter 12

ON THE BRINK

I couldn't wait for school to finish that day. I kept my head down for the rest of the day. I stayed away from Tina. I stayed away from all second years.

Robyn and Rebecca were very good to me. They hung out with me all day, they talked to me at break time and they had lunch with me at lunch time. I felt visible, vulnerable. I felt as though the whole school was looking at me, talking about me, laughing at me as I queued to get my lunch. The girl who couldn't stand up to Tina Kane. The girl who was too scared to fight Tina Kane.

I was on the brink of tears all day.

I was very happy when school was over but when I got home all I wanted to do was stay there. Stay in my room. I didn't want to come down for dinner and I definitely didn't want to go to training that evening.

I had dinner though, and I went to training. Mum dropped me down. I didn't tell her what had happened at school. Firstly, there would be nothing that she could do to make the situation better. Secondly, she would want to do something, and anything that she would do would only make things worse. Thirdly, she would worry about me, and I didn't want her to worry about me.

'Are you okay, pet?' she asked as we pulled into the car park beside the pitch.

'Yes Mum,' I said.

I could feel her looking at me. I looked up at her and she was smiling.

'What?' I asked, a little more abruptly than I had intended.

'Are you doing okay?' she asked. 'It's hard for you, isn't it?

'I'm fine, Mum,' I said.

'It will get better,' she said. 'It will never be easy, but it will get less hard as time goes on.'

'I know,' I said.

I sat there for a few seconds. I wanted to throw my whole body into Mum's arms and bawl, but that wouldn't have solved anything. I could feel my eyes welling up, so I opened the car door.

'See you later,' I said, and I climbed out of the car without looking back at Mum.

'Enjoy training,' she called after me.

Stephen wasn't there and Patrick launched into running from the start. I thought that we would start off by talking about Sunday's match, but we didn't. It was as though we hadn't had a match on Sunday. We didn't talk about it at all, we didn't talk about the positives to be taken from it or the negatives from which we could learn, and there was no easing off in Patrick's training to allow for the fact that we had had a game the previous day.

'Red cone and back,' said Patrick. 'White cone and back, blue cone and back. Sprint. All the way. Go!'

'Aw Patrick,' said Shelley. 'We had a match yesterday. Go easy on us.'

'When I was your age,' said Patrick, 'I used to walk ten miles to play a game, then walk ten miles home again. And I'd be out working on the farm later that evening. Now give me twenty push-ups.'

'Ah, Patrick!' protested Shelley. 'Really?'

'Do it!'

He was serious, and Shelley did it.

I was fine doing the shuttles. I was fast and I was fit and I didn't mind. I just didn't like the standing around between exercises, because I didn't really have anyone to talk to. Robyn had Rebecca. Aoife had Sofia. If only Sally was here.

Debbie was nice to me, but she usually partnered with Lily. Tina had Sinéad and Edel and just about everybody else. Robyn and Rebecca did include me, but when it came to partnering up, they were with each other and I was with Patrick.

And I was still disappointed that we didn't get to talk about Sunday's match.

Training ended with a game. Training must always end with a game, in every club, in every corner of the country, at every level. I didn't play well. I didn't feel confident. I felt meek.

The thing with Tina that morning was on my mind. That was unusual. When I am playing football, normally all that matters is what's going on within the confines of the pitch. I can usually block out what is happening in the rest of my life. I can concentrate completely on what is going on between the four white lines.

Not that evening though. Not in that training game.

It didn't help that I was marking Tina. I felt intimidated by her. When she had the ball or when she called for the ball or when she shot or when she passed. I didn't want to mark her. I didn't want to be near her.

'Stay out of my way or you're dead,' she said to me as we waited for Sofia to kick the ball out in our direction.

So I did. She won that ball and she won every other ball.

I didn't call for the ball and I felt nervous when I got it. We were only playing for fifteen or twenty minutes, during which time I got the ball six or seven times, and I'd say I gave it away five or six times.

I was glad when Patrick blew the final whistle.

'Okay girls, well done,' he said. 'See you all on Wednesday.'

As I made my way towards the gate, I thought I heard Patrick calling after me, but I wasn't sure, so I kept walking.

'Anna!'

It was definitely Patrick calling after me all right. I turned around.

'Are you okay?' he asked.

'Yes,' I said, a bit hesitantly.

Patrick had never spoken to me one-on-one before.

'I'm fine,' I assured him.

'Okay,' said Patrick. 'See you on Wednesday.'

I went out the gate and into the car park. There was Mum, in her car, with her window down and Stephen beside the window, laughing. I opened the passenger door and got in.

'Hi Anna,' said Stephen. 'How was training?'

'Fine,' I said.

I'm not sure that he really heard me, nor that he really cared how training had been. He quickly resumed his conversation with Mum.

'So I won't be doing that again anyway,' he said, and the two of them laughed.

'I'll bet you won't,' said Mum.

'Okay, thanks, Stephen,' she said as she started the car. 'See you on Wednesday.'

☣ ☣ ☣

I had a shower when I got home and got into my navy pyjamas. They were my Christmas pyjamas. It said ''Tis the season to be sleepy' on the front, emblazoned in red and white letters, but I didn't care. They were cosy. They were my cosiest pyjamas, so they were my pyjamas of choice any night that it was cold, which was pretty much every night in Granny and Grandad's house.

My laundry was on my bed when I got back into my bedroom. My jeans, my favourite orange top, my Ed Sheeran t-shirt, my football gear: white shorts, black training jersey, tracksuit top, orange socks. I picked up the orange socks from the top of the pile. Mum had half tucked them together, so that the feet were dangling together out of the little rolled up ball of sock. I rubbed one of the feet against my face, and I thought of Daddy.

It wasn't fair. Why me? Everybody else had a dad. Orla had a dad, Robyn and Rebecca had dads. Even Hannah back in Galway had a dad, even if he wasn't a very nice dad, even if he used to make you feel a little bit scared, even if there was a different atmosphere in Hannah's house when he was there, when he wasn't 'on a job' or in the pub, which made you not want to be there. I hadn't spoken to Hannah in ages. Just shows you, when you move house, when you move away from somewhere. Everyone is so busy. Must text Hannah.

Even stupid Tina had a dad. Stephen. And it seemed like he was a good dad, a nice dad. Tina didn't deserve a good dad. She was so mean. Tina didn't have a mum though. Well, she did have a mum. Just that her dad and her mum were not together. Maybe that was her bad thing. Maybe everybody has some bad thing.

The thing was, I had had the best dad in the world. Really. Maybe everybody says that. I can't imagine that Hannah would say that, but maybe most people say that they have the best dad in the world. They couldn't have though, because I had. And I knew it then. When he was alive. I didn't need for him to be taken away from me for me to know that.

He was brilliant. He would have done anything for me, for us. For Charlie and me, and for Mum. I felt so safe when he was there. I hated it if he left the house in the morning before I went to school, and I loved it when I heard his car pulling up in the driveway when he arrived home, or when I heard his keys rattling in the front door. And when he went away for a few days for work, which was rare, I counted down the days until he would come home.

I loved playing football with him, and I loved it when he helped me with my Maths homework, and I loved it when he tickled me. I hated it and I loved it. I used to shriek before he did. And run away. But I still wanted him to tickle me. Delicious fear, Daddy called it.

I loved when we all played Boggle together, and I loved watching football with him, or rugby, or *Friends*, or the News. Well, not so much the News. The News was boring and usually bad. They should call it The Bad News.

I loved it when he made up his after-dinner quizzes. He'd have questions for me and for Charlie and for Mum. Different questions, questions with different levels of difficulty. Like, he'd ask me what was the longest river in Europe, or who the Taoiseach was. He'd ask Charlie something ridiculous, like what was three minus one. He had to give Charlie easy questions, because Charlie used to get very upset if he didn't know the answer. And he'd ask Mum something difficult, like what was the capital of Uruguay, and Mum would go mad!

It's Montevideo.

I loved surprising Daddy with a cup of coffee. The delight on his face. If he was in his office, deep in thought or on his computer, I loved making a cup of coffee and just bringing it in to him. He loved coffee. It didn't matter what time of the day it was, or when he had had his previous cup of coffee, he always loved a cup of coffee, and he always hugged me and kissed me lots when I brought one into him.

I loved going to the beach with him. We'd just walk on the beach and talk about stuff. We talked about God a bit, and we counted our blessings. Daddy used to talk about how great it was that Granny and Grandad were doing so well, that they were so healthy and young, and about how lucky we were, to have each other, the four of us. How lucky we were that we were all so healthy and happy, and that he had a job that allowed him spend so much time with us, and that we were doing so well in school, and at football, and that we lived in such a nice place, and that Charlie and I had such good friends. He used to say that we should always try to appreciate how lucky we were when things were going well.

I wasn't sure about God any more. If God was so good, why did he take Daddy from me?

Maybe there was a reason. Maybe God needed Daddy for something. Maybe somebody else needed him more than I needed him. I couldn't imagine that that could be the case though. I couldn't imagine that anybody could need Daddy more than I needed him. I hadn't spoken to God in a while.

My eyes were welling up as I took the orange socks apart. I held one in my left hand and one in my right hand. There couldn't be something in them, could there?

I started to put them on. I wasn't thinking. I put on the left one first, as usual. I put it over my left toes, onto my left foot and pulled it all the way up under the leg of my pyjamas, up to my knee. Then I folded down the top of the sock, so that the new top of the sock sat just below my kneecap.

I did the same with the right sock. Up to my knee, then tucked it down.

I had this strange feeling. I was still sad, but I didn't feel like crying. I felt assured in a weird way. Like, that Daddy was there with me, in the room, watching me, smiling, telling me not to be sad or scared. I just sat there for a few minutes, trying to figure out how I felt. It was a peculiar feeling. I wasn't happy, but I wasn't sad. I felt safe. Content.

The door of my bedroom opened and Mum walked in. She looked at me, sitting on the bed, hair all wet, pyjamas rolled up, orange socks on my feet, pulled up to my knees. She looked at my face, then looked at my feet, then looked at my face again. I felt a little bit sheepish, a little embarrassed.

Mum just smiled.

Chapter 13

'NICE DUTCH BRAIDS'

I could hear the hum coming from the open door of the classroom as I approached. There was usually a hum from the classroom, but it seemed to be louder than usual. More excited. Maybe I was later than normal. Maybe there were just more people in than there usually are when I get in.

I walked in through the open door and made my way to the coat racks without really looking up or looking at anyone or looking for anyone. I didn't really have a best friend to look for anyway, or a group of friends. I put my bag on the floor and, as I took off my coat and went to hang it up, I could sense that the hum was getting quieter. The noise reduced until there was almost complete silence. It was weird.

'Nice Dutch braids!' someone shouted, and everybody laughed.

It was only then that I looked up and saw that everyone was looking at me. Most people were smiling. What the hell? I could feel myself going red. What was going on? I had my hair in a bobbin, not in Dutch braids. I picked up my bag and made my way to my desk. I sat down and started to get my Irish books out of my bag.

The noise level started to pick up again. I was relieved about that. They didn't appear to be talking about me either, which was good. Then Miss Donnelly came in. It was always a relief when the teacher came in. It meant that class could start and it wasn't obvious that I had nobody to talk to. It was the same feeling I would get when training actually started, when the pre-training banter – of which I wasn't really a part – had to end.

Nice Dutch braids? What was that all about?

I was opening my sandwich at break time when Robyn and Rebecca came over to me.

'Hi Anna,' said Robyn.

'Hi Robyn,' I said. 'Hi Rebecca.'

They came as a pair. Like Timon and Pumbaa.

'Hi Anna,' said Rebecca. 'Are you okay?'

'Yeah,' I said. 'Just hungry! Do either of you want half a sandwich?'

'No thanks,' said Robyn.

'So, you sure you're okay?' Rebecca asked again.

I looked back at her, probably blankly. I thought I had already answered that one. They were very nice, and I appreciated the fact that they came over to talk to me, I really did. But sometimes, Rebecca wasn't the brightest.

'About the post?' she said.

Another blank look.

'The Instagram post? Tina's Instagram post?'

Now I felt like *I* wasn't the brightest.

Robyn nudged Rebecca.

'I told you that she wouldn't know,' she said, as if I wasn't there. I presumed that the 'she' was me.

They both looked at me sympathetically. Pityingly. Poor Anna. I knew that they meant well. I didn't ask. I assumed that they would tell me.

'Tina posted something on Instagram last night,' said Robyn softly. 'Did you not see it?'

'I'm not on Instagram,' I said.

'You're not on Instagram?' asked Rebecca.

She was quite incredulous.

'What are you on then? Snapchat?'

I shook my head.

'Facebook?'

I shook my head.

'Twitter?'

'I can save you some time here, Rebecca,' I said. 'I'm not on social media. I'm on WhatsApp. Does that count?'

Again, pitying looks. Apparently, WhatsApp is not social media.

'So what did Tina post?' I asked.

Of course, I wanted to know.

'It wasn't that bad,' said Robyn. 'We'd show you if we were allowed to use our phones in school, but it wasn't that bad. Really.'

'It was a picture of you,' said Rebecca. 'Years ago. I'd say you're about five or six in the picture. In a ballet dress and ballet shoes. A big smile on your face. You look so cute!'

'And Dutch braids?' I asked.

The two girls nodded.

I knew the photograph well. It was taken at some ballet dancing competition that I won when I was small, and it appeared in the *Connacht Tribune*. It was a big deal at the time. I was delighted. My picture in the *Connacht Tribune*. And actually, I was eight.

'She wrote something too,' said Rebecca. 'Something

like, she should have stuck to ballet because she can't play football.'

'There aren't many comments though,' said Robyn.

'No,' said Rebecca. 'There are a few at the start, people asking who it is. People guessing. Then Tina says that it's you, and there are only a few more comments after that. Smiley faces and things.'

I could feel myself going red again. The centre of attention again. I hated being the centre of attention. Even if it was online, even if I hadn't been aware of it. And it had happened the previous evening, so it didn't make sense that I was only getting embarrassed about it now.

'It's not so bad,' said Robyn. 'Really.'

Of the pair of them, of Robyn and Rebecca, I was quickly figuring out, Robyn spoke the most sense. And she was right, it wasn't so bad. It could have been a lot worse. There were photographs of me in the drawer at home that were way worse. I guess that this one was the worst one that Tina could find. It was probably the only one of me that was on the internet.

Even so, it was upsetting. Not that there was a picture of eight-year-old me in a ballet costume on the internet, all smiles and everything. Strangely, I didn't really mind that. I wasn't embarrassed by the fact that

I did ballet when I was smaller or that I won a prize or that my picture appeared in the *Connacht Tribune*. I quite liked ballet, I enjoyed doing it. I only gave it up because it clashed with football and, actually, I think that it helped my football, my balance.

The upsetting thing was that Tina posted it, that she had wanted to upset me, and, if Robyn and Rebecca were right, that she had said that I couldn't play football.

The feeling was with me all day. It sat in the pit of my stomach.

I Facetimed Sally that evening and told her about Tina. I told her all about her, about the football and the incident in the school and the Instagram post. I felt comfortable telling Sally about it, more comfortable than I would have felt about telling my mum. I'm not sure why. Maybe I was afraid that Mum would worry about me or that she would want to do something about it, that she would want to fix it. And she couldn't fix it. If she tried to do something about it, I was sure that she would make it worse.

Also, I think that I wanted to appear to my mum to be strong, to let her think that everything was good with me, that I was getting on well at school. Not that I was struggling every day, that I dreaded going in every morning, that I had no real friends, no best friend, no group of friends to which I felt I belonged.

I could always be myself with Sally. I could tell her stuff and she wouldn't judge me, or want to do something about it. She just made things seem better than I thought they were. Not that she said anything really. She just listened and nodded and smiled.

It wasn't all about Tina either. We spoke about school and Miss Donnelly and Sally's mum's intention to give up smoking, and Charlie's love of peanut butter, and Alan's obsession with cars.

It was good to talk to Sally. I felt much better going to bed that evening.

Chapter 14

BIG GAME

I took a deep breath and pushed open the dressing room door. I always felt nervous when I first arrived somewhere. Anywhere. School, training, a party. I was the new arrival, so I was sure that everyone who was already there would be looking at me. And who would I talk to first? Everybody who was already there would be already talking to somebody. What if there was nobody left to talk to me?

The first thing that hit me was the smell of Deep Heat. Even before I walked into the dressing room. Stephen loved Deep Heat. The girls loved Deep Heat. They smothered their legs with it before matches. The bigger the match, it seemed to me, the more Deep Heat they used.

This was a big match, the championship quarter-final, against Tullafin. Tullafin were a good club, they had a good set up and they had a good senior team, but their under-age teams were usually beatable. Stephen said that that was because their under-age coaches weren't as good as our under-age coaches.

Most of the girls were there when I walked in. There was a good hum of excitement mixed in with the smell of Deep Heat. The girls were in varying states of readiness, some with their shorts on, some still in their clothes, as I anxiously sought a space on the seats where I could sit. Not in Tina's corner anyway, where she and Sinéad and Edel hung out. They always commandeered the back left corner of the dressing room. There was a semi-space between Orla and Robyn, so I headed for that.

'Hi, Anna,' said Orla. 'You good?'

Immediately I felt so much better.

'Hi, Orla,' I said. 'I am. All set! You?'

'Yeah, sure let's give it a go.'

Robyn smiled and moved some of her stuff towards her to make plenty of room for me to sit down. I was getting to like Robyn more and more. Rebecca stretched her fisted hand across Robyn in my direction. For an instant, I didn't know what she was doing. I thought she was threatening me for some reason. I must have had a puzzled look on my face.

'Fist-bump,' she explained.

I bumped her fist with my fist and smiled. She was nice too, Rebecca. She was a little ditzy and a bit silly sometimes, but she was nice. She meant well.

I started to get ready. Black shorts, green socks. Left sock first, right sock second. And boots. Left boot first, right boot second.

There was a knock on the door, and Stephen and Patrick and Orla's mum walked in.

'Okay girls,' said Stephen, as the hum got a little quieter. Still some girls were talking though.

'Here!' shouted Patrick, not happy that the noise level had not reduced to zero. 'Listen up now!'

Stephen smiled and started talking.

'Right, now, I don't need to tell you how important this game is. The quarter-final of the championship. Lose this, and we're out. Win it, and we're into the semi-final. And we can win it. If we play to our potential, we can win it. Now, I'm going to name the team and then we can have a chat after that.'

He started calling out names and throwing out jerseys. Sofia was number one of course. Rebecca two, Robyn three, Edel four. I was hoping that I would be on the team. I expected that I would be, I had played well in the last match and I thought that I was worth my place, but you never know until you are named. You can't take it for granted that you are going to be starting.

'Debbie,' said Stephen as he threw a jersey to Debbie beside me.

'Right half-forward.'

Number 10.

'Sinéad,' he said as he threw the number 11 jersey to Sinéad, beside Tina, who was busy putting on her number nine jersey.

'On the forty.'

He looked around the room and his eyes settled on me and my heart did a little somersault.

'Anna,' he said as he threw a jersey to me. 'Left half-forward.'

Wow! Starting at left half-forward, further out the pitch than left full-forward and more involved in the play. I was delighted. Stephen had enough faith in me to give me a position that should see me more involved. That's how I interpreted it anyway. Maybe he was moving me further away from the goals because he didn't think that I was accurate in my shooting, but I doubted that.

I didn't hear the next few positions. I was too busy getting my head around the fact that, firstly, I was on the starting 15, and then that I was left half-forward, not left full-forward. I tuned back in as Stephen was handing out the last of the jerseys.

'Amanda, full-forward. On the square. Shelley, left-corner.'

He threw the number 15 jersey to Shelley, who looked disappointed. She had been moved from left half-forward to left full-forward. Stephen had swapped her with me. But she was still starting, so I didn't feel bad for her. Not too bad anyway. By the time I tuned back in again, Stephen was talking.

'Lily and Tina,' he was saying. 'In midfield. If one of you goes back to defend, the other must stay in midfield. And if one of you goes forward to attack, the other must stay in midfield. We must hold midfield at all times. I know you know this, but there were times, against Croughton, when you both went forward.'

'That was just a challenge match,' Tina interrupted.

'It doesn't matter,' Stephen said sharply. 'It was a match. We need to play our game every time. Even in challenges. And today, we need to make sure that we get it right, okay?'

He looked at Tina. She just met his gaze. She didn't say anything.

'I don't want to see both of you going forward at the same time.'

Lily nodded. Tina just stared back, blankly. His daughter.

Stephen spoke for about fifteen minutes. Sofia, always look to give short kick-outs. Full-backs and half-backs, look to get free for the quick kick-out. And stay tight when we are defending. Full-forwards, stay forward, almost on the end line. Half-forwards, lots of running. Shoot when the shot is on. Pass when it isn't.

'Right, let's get out there!'

I was excited. Excited and nervous. There was a nice feeling about the place. As warm as a summer's evening, a Thursday evening, and there were plenty of people around the pitch. And it was a home game for us. That helped. But still I was nervous. I was anxious that I would play well, for me and for the team, and for Stephen. That he wouldn't regret moving me to left half-forward.

I tried to get tuned in. I went over to the dressing room goals. I went behind them and put my hands on the fence.

'Are you ready?'

'I am.

'Tuned in?'

'Tuned in.'

'Focused on the pitch?'

'Focused on the pitch.'

'Take responsibility.'

'Take responsibility.'

'Do your best.'

I closed my eyes and tried to feel Daddy's hands on my head and his kiss on my forehead, but it wasn't easy. It wasn't easy to concentrate. It wasn't easy to block out the noise around me.

'What's that girl doing?' I heard a little girl ask.

'She's concentrating,' said a man's voice.

'Who is that?' asked an old man's voice.

'That's Emma Murtagh's girl,' said another old man's voice.

'Is it really?' asked the first old man's voice.

It was impossible to concentrate.

'Anna!'

Stephen was calling me over. The warm-up passing drills had started, so I joined in. Catch, hand-pass, move, catch, hand-pass, move. Join the back of the line.

Tina won the toss, and chose to play with the slight

breeze for the first half, into the river goals. We gathered in a circle with arms around each other.

'Who are we?' shouted Tina.

'Ballymarra!' everyone shouted back. It caught me a bit unawares. I just joined in the 'marra' part, and quite softly.

'Who are we?' Tina shouted again, a little more loudly.

'Ballymarra!' everyone shouted, also more loudly. I joined in this one, but I wasn't as loud as the others.

'Who are we?' Tina shouted at the top of her voice.

'Ballymarra! Ballymarra! Ballymarra!'

I put in my mouth guard and took my place on the pitch, left half-forward. I looked down towards the river goals, but there was nothing behind them. No shadow. I wasn't expecting to see anything anyway. I looked back up to our goals, the road goals. I wasn't expecting to see anything there either. Really I wasn't. But I looked anyway, just in case. No shadow.

Tina won the throw-in and went forward. Lily got free and Tina passed it to her. I got behind my marker and called.

'Lily!'

Lily kicked the ball towards me with the inside of her right boot. It bounced once as it travelled into my path. Perfect pace, perfect pass, I didn't even have to break stride. I could gather it in my chest, around thirty metres from goal, and kick it over the bar.

I had half an eye on the goals as I went to catch the ball. There they were, a little to my left, gleaming white, inviting, nobody between me and them. I was readying myself for my shot before I had the ball in my hands.

The ball hit my chest and went forward before I had my hands in place to secure it. It hit my right hand and went beyond it. I stretched my left hand out to try to recover it, but not on time. It had escaped from my grasp by the time one of the Tullafin girls grabbed it and hit me on the shoulder with her shoulder. I fell to the ground, winced with the pain and the disappointment as the Tullafin girl cleared the ball up the field.

'Anna you're useless!' shouted Tina.

That set the tone for me. Nothing went right. The Tullafin number five beat me to every 50–50 ball and some 60–40 balls and some 70–30 balls. And the balls that I did get, I didn't use very well. My passing was awful, I gave it to Tullafin as often as I found one of my own players, and I kicked two wides and no points.

On the plus side, we were two points ahead when the half-time whistle was blown, 0–6 to 0–4.

Stephen gave his usual half-time team-talk. He always focused on the positives at half-time. He always encouraged at half-time. And he had a few tactical changes. Amanda had the measure of their full-back, so let the ball in earlier to her. The short kick-outs weren't working, so Sofia was going to kick long in the second half, with the breeze. And I was going in left full-forward. Shelley was coming back out, left half-forward.

'Okay, same effort this half girls,' shouted Stephen. 'Let's go!'

Before I could get back onto the pitch, Stephen called me.

'Is everything okay?' he asked me.

'Yes,' I said softly.

Besides the fact that I had a nightmare first half. I didn't say that. I didn't need to say it. He knew that.

'Okay,' he said. 'In this half, in the corner, stay close to the end line. Use the end line as your starting position, start with your back to the end line, so that you can face the play. Use your speed to come out and get the ball. Then you'll be closer to goal than in the first half. Use your accurate shooting. Okay?'

I nodded.

The second half didn't go any better for me. I hugged the end line, like Stephen had told me to, but my marker just stood in front of me and beat me to the first two balls. The third ball that came in went over her head, I caught it and kicked it wide. The next ball, I got as well, but I deliberated too long, unsure if I should shoot or pass to Shelley, who was free. The Tullafin girl punched the ball out of my hands and cleared it. And still no shadow behind the goals.

Two minutes later, Stephen took me off. He was right to take me off. I was awful.

'Anna!' he shouted from the sideline.

It's the call that you hate getting.

Aoife put her right hand out as she ran onto the field, and I touched it with my right hand. Stephen threw a tracksuit top to me as I sat down in the dug-out.

'Well done Anna,' he said.

He couldn't have meant it.

My own performance aside, the game went very well for us. We scored three of the first four points in the second half, and then we got a goal. I thought that Sinéad was going for a point, but it fell short and dropped over the Tullafin goalkeeper's head into the net. That put us seven points clear, and they were never going to catch us after that. We won by nine.

It was all celebrations afterwards. Everybody was delighted. No Ballymarra girls' team had ever got to the county final, and we were into the semi-final now, just one game away from the final. I found it difficult to join in the celebrations. I found it difficult to be in celebratory mood. I knew that I had played terribly, that I hadn't contributed to the victory at all. When people said well done, I just smiled.

I felt hollow. I was happy that we had won, happy for the girls, happy that I was on the team that was now in the semi-final. But I still felt empty. Unfulfilled. And I felt sad.

Whenever I had a bad game, Daddy would always console me. He always knew exactly what to say. Mum was great, but she didn't have the same understanding. She would say things like, it just didn't happen for you today, you'll be better next time. Or, you did your best love, and that's all you can do. Or, the worst, I thought you played well. That's the last thing you want to hear when you know that you have played terribly.

Daddy had an understanding, and he had a way of phrasing things. He had been at the game, always, he would know that I had had a bad game, but he would also know what I had done well, and he would focus on those things. Specifics. I would always feel better about my performance after talking with Daddy. I would always be able to take something positive out of it. At the end of our chat, I would always be bursting to play the next game. I would always be looking forward to the next opportunity, when I could play better, when I could put it right.

The way I felt after the quarter-final though, I never wanted to play football again, and I knew that there was going to be no chat with Daddy. No talk that would make me feel better.

I missed Daddy. I missed Daddy so much.

I just wanted to get out of there. Some of the girls were going into the village for chips later on, and Robyn and Rebecca asked me if I was going, but that was the last thing I wanted to do. I quickly said good-bye and came home in the car with Mum.

Chapter 15

• • • • • •

NOT A DATE

I was half way down the stairs when Grandad called from the sitting room.

'Can someone get the door?'

It usually took longer than it should for someone to open the front door after the door bell had rung.

'Shhhh!' said Granny in a hushed shout. 'You'll wake the baby.'

Charlie was always going to be the baby.

'I'm getting it Granny,' I whisper-shouted.

Before I got to the bottom of the stairs I could see that it was a man. The silhouette behind the frosted glass was that of a man. A tall man, probably wearing a dark jacket. I opened the door carefully.

'Hi, Anna,' said the man.

'Stephen?' I said. I thought I had hidden my surprise and my disappointment, but I wasn't sure.

My mind raced. He was here to tell me how badly I had played. That he could see now that Tina was right, that I wasn't a good player at all. That the standard in Wicklow was way higher than the standard in Galway, and that I wasn't good enough here.

Or that he was dropping me from the team. I had played so badly earlier, there was no way back for me. He couldn't see how I would fit in, or recover my place.

Or my thing with Tina. Stephen's daughter. The star player on the team. Either I had to leave the team or Tina had to leave the team, and Tina wasn't leaving the team.

'How are you?' asked Stephen.

'I'm okay,' I said.

I looked at him, expecting him to speak. He was the adult after all. He looked back at me, a little nervously.

Looked like it was up to me.

'I was awful earlier,' I said.

'No you weren't,' said Stephen. 'You didn't have one of your better games. That happens. You can't always be brilliant.'

I nodded. I didn't believe him though. He wasn't very convincing, that I wasn't awful.

So I just stood there, looking at Stephen, in my pyjamas, ''Tis the season to be sleepy', holding the door with my right hand, half-leaning against it. For support.

He just stood there in the porch, looking at me, half-smiling, nervous, uneasy. What did he want? I probably should have asked him but I didn't. That wasn't really my place. In adult-kid conversations, it's usually the adult who runs the conversation. That has always been my expectation anyway.

'Stephen!' I heard Mum's voice behind me, on her way down the stairs.

Stephen suddenly lit up. He didn't have to be dealing with this awkward kid any more. He mumbled something like, 'Emma', or, 'Hi Emma'.

'Are you not letting Stephen in Anna?' asked Mum, half for Stephen I was sure, only half for me. 'Are you going to leave Stephen out there on the porch for the whole evening?'

Mum was laughing.

'I didn't know if he wanted to come in or not,' I said.

'Well, how are you going to know if you don't ask him?' said Mum, looking at Stephen and smiling.

I hated when Mum did that, said something to me,

but looked at the adult. She wasn't saying it to me or for me at all, she was saying it for the adult. To be funny.

It worked. Stephen laughed.

I left the front door and went into the kitchen. Stephen and Mum followed me in, telling each other how well they each looked.

Mum did look well. It was only when we got into the kitchen that I noticed. She had nice make-up on, her hair looked nice, her eyebrows were good, and she was wearing her good jeans and a really nice cream top that I had never seen before. And her cool red shoes that I wanted.

'Are you going out?' I asked.

'I am, pet. I told you yesterday, remember?'

I did remember. But I had forgotten.

'Where are you going?'

'We're just going out for a drink.'

'With who?' I asked.

'With whom?' she said.

I hated it when she did that too.

'With whom,' I repeated, drawing out the 'whom' and making a face at the same time.

'With Stephen,' she said simply.

It took me a second or two to figure it out. I just stood there in silence as my brain clicked into gear. A drink with Stephen. Just Stephen. She didn't say with the gang or with the girls or that Stephen was just coming along or just giving her a lift.

Stephen was suitably quiet and sheepish-looking. It wasn't like him. I was used to him being in charge and talking tactics and shouting directions from the sideline. I wasn't used to this Stephen. Sheepish Stephen. Quiet Stephen. Shy Stephen. I didn't like this Stephen.

'Like, a date?' I asked.

'Well, I wouldn't call it a date,' said Mum, laughing. 'Would you Stephen?'

'No,' said Stephen quietly. 'Not a date. Definitely not a date.'

'We're just going for a drink,' said Mum. 'Just two old friends going for a drink. Just to catch up.'

'Where are you going?' I asked.

I couldn't think of anything else to say. In truth, I didn't care where they were going. But I couldn't say what I wanted to say. That Mum shouldn't be going for a drink with Stephen or with anyone. That she was Daddy's wife and she was my mother and Charlie's mother, and what business did she have going out for a drink with Stephen or with anyone? Going on a date. Even if it wasn't a date.

And it probably was a date anyway. New top, cool

jeans, red shoes. And Stephen was wearing a shirt and a jacket. I don't think I'd ever seen him in anything other than a tracksuit top before.

It wasn't even a nice jacket. It was one of those horrible tweed jackets, probably with patches on the elbows. I couldn't see his elbows. It looked like it was made out of a blanket, one of those blankets that itches your chin if you accidentally rub it, if you don't have the sheet stretched out over it and doubled down so that your chin rubs off the sheet, not the blanket.

'Brogan's,' said Mum.

'What?' I asked, brought back to reality, back from my runaway thoughts of blankets.

'Brogan's,' said Mum again.

I stared at her blankly.

'We're going to Brogan's,' said Mum.

'Why not Mister Fogg's?' I asked, still a bit dazed.

I had never even heard of Brogan's.

'Don't you always go to Mister Fogg's?'

'Sometimes,' said Mum. 'On the odd occasion on which I do go out. That's where the girls usually go. Which is why we're going to Brogan's!'

She looked at Stephen and laughed. She was doing it again. Stephen laughed back. Stephen was in a laughy, nervy mood. If Mum had told him that the cat had been hit by a car, I'm sure that he would have laughed.

'Would you like to have a drink here before we go?' asked Mum.

'Whatever you want, Ems,' said Stephen.

Ems? Seriously? Stephen? Nobody called my mum Ems except Daddy and Granny and Grandad and maybe Brenda sometimes. I had never heard anyone else in Ballymarra calling her Ems. Ems? I was liking this Stephen less and less.

'I'm easy,' Stephen continued. 'Honestly.'

'Hi, Stephen.'

I could hear Granny's voice from the hall before she came into the kitchen.

'Hi, Mrs Murtagh,' said Stephen.

'Oh, don't you look smart,' Granny said as Stephen gave her an awkward kiss on the cheek.

'Doesn't Stephen look smart, Anna?'

Depends on your definition of smart, Granny.

'Yes he does,' I said.

Nobody spoke for about a second and a half, but it felt like about a year and a half.

'I think we'll just go, Stephen,' said Mum. 'Will we?'

'Okay, Emma,' Stephen said.

We were back to Emma. Maybe it was because Granny had arrived into the room, or maybe it was because Stephen had forgotten himself a little when he had said Ems. Or maybe he had thought that he would float the Ems thing, just to see how it would go, if it felt comfortable or not, and that he had decided that it didn't really work. Maybe be had seen my reaction. Maybe my thoughts had influenced my facial expression and he had seen it. Or maybe I was reading too much into it all.

Before I knew what was happening, Mum was kissing me and hugging me and telling me to look after Granny and telling Granny to look after me, and telling us both not to be eating too much chocolate or drinking too much wine. That was another joke for Stephen.

Mum then gave Granny a kiss and told her that she wouldn't be too late and that Charlie should be okay, that he should sleep all night and that, if he woke up, just to sing him a few lines of 'Lullaby and Goodnight', like she used to do with her.

Stephen gave Granny a kiss, and there was an awkward moment, just a fraction of a second, when I thought that he was going to give me a kiss. I think I would have died, or run away, or kicked him. One of the three. Thankfully, if he thought about it, he thought better of it, he decided not to. He just said goodnight to me and said something about needing my sleep for my energy levels for football or something. Something that he didn't really mean. Just a throwaway something so that he could say something to me.

Then they were gone out the door and I was in floods of tears.

Chapter 16

NOT GETTING EASIER

Granny smelt like Granny always smells: a mixture of wool and perfume and old person. I loved how Granny smelt. I could hardly breathe, my head was buried so deeply into her chest, but I didn't care. Her perfume was not strong, just a hint of White Linen, and it was nice.

'Stephen is not trying to replace your daddy,' Granny was saying. 'That's the last thing that he wants to do.'

I didn't say anything. I just continued to sob, audibly, uncontrollably. I could feel Granny's cardigan getting wetter with my tears, I could feel the wet wool against my face.

I didn't care whether Stephen was or wasn't trying to replace Daddy. It didn't matter if he was trying. He wouldn't do it. He couldn't. Nobody could. Not for me, not for Charlie. Daddy would always be my daddy. Stephen wouldn't be. Ever.

But he could marry Mum, and that wouldn't be good. He could move in with us, or we could move in with him, or we could all move in together. Me and Mum and Charlie and Stephen and Tina. Imagine that. Tina would be my sister. I would have to share a bathroom with her and maybe even a bedroom, and she would be there at breakfast and at dinner and at bedtime, and she would steal my clothes and my shampoo and my books. Well, maybe she wouldn't steal my books. I doubt that Tina had ever stolen anybody's books.

But that wasn't really the issue. I consoled myself with the thought that, if that happened, it wouldn't happen for years, and I could be in college or working or any-where. The issue was now. What was happening now? Mum and Stephen had gone out for a drink. Mum was happy and giddy and showy-offy. With Stephen.

Nothing about this was good. Mum was never like that with Daddy. She was never showy-offy. She was always just herself. She always said that Daddy was good for her. She told me once that she was a better person when she was with Daddy than she was when she wasn't with him.

I remember one time Mum was telling Evelyn's mum that she had met Bono. It was a small insignificant thing, but it stuck out in my mind at the time. Sometimes you remember things that were small and insignificant at the time. They just stay with you for some reason and you remember them years later.

Mum often puts on a little bit of a posh accent when she is trying to impress people. Mum didn't know Evelyn's mum very well at the time, but she asked her to stay for a cup of tea this day when she was collecting Evelyn from our house. I wasn't very old at the time, five or six or seven. I didn't really know who Bono was, but I did know that he was important.

I remember that Evelyn and I were lying on the floor, on the rug, playing 'Guess Who?', and Charlie and Daddy were on the couch, playing Peekaboo. (Charlie loved playing Peekaboo. It didn't matter how often he saw Daddy's face appearing from behind the book, he laughed his little full-face laugh every time.) Mum and Evelyn's mum were sitting at the counter top, drinking tea and probably eating Mikados or Fig Rolls, when Mum told Evelyn's mum, in her slightly posh accent, that she had met Bono. I remember, because I remember hearing her say it, and I remember thinking, that's cool, Mum met Bono. I wonder what Bono does.

A little while later, Evelyn's mum said, we must be going, we've stayed long enough. Thanks a million Emma for having her. Bye, Jack. Bye, Anna. Bye, little Charlie. Come on Ev.

'Who was your guy?' I asked Evelyn.

'Anna, Evelyn has to go,' said Mum.

'Richard,' said Evelyn.

A man. Again. She had chosen a man in every game that we had played.

'Do you always choose a man?' I asked.

'Evelyn, come on,' said Evelyn's mum.

'Yes,' said Evelyn. 'There are more men. If you choose a woman and if they ask you if it's a man or a woman, it's easy for them to guess it.'

I learned something that day. Basic 'Guess Who?' strategy. Always choose a man.

I went out to the hall with Mum to say bye to Evelyn and her mum. When we came back into the kitchen, Daddy was lying on the couch with Charlie on his tummy and a big grin on his face.

'What?' asked Mum, as I sat down on the rug and started to tidy up 'Guess Who?' Evelyn had chosen Richard all right.

'Nothing,' said Daddy, still grinning.

I started to count the characters in 'Guess Who?' Nineteen men and only five women. Evelyn was right. I hadn't copped that before. Although, you couldn't be certain with some of them. For example, it looked like Peter was wearing lipstick. I suppose his name was a giveaway though. Definitely a man. And George. He always looked a bit feminine to me. And you could even argue that he had a girl's name. Like George in the Famous Five.

'No, there's something,' said Mum, smiling. 'What is it?'

The conversation went something like this:

Daddy (small smile): 'You really met Bono?'

Short silence.

Mum (posh accent): 'Yes. I met Bono.'

Another short silence.

Daddy (big smile): 'Really?'

Slightly longer silence.

Mum (slightly sheepish, posh accent): 'Well, he said hello to me.'

Daddy (small laugh): 'Did he?'

Mum (normal accent): 'Yes. Yes he did.'

Daddy (big laugh): 'Or was he just in the same room as you once? At a reception?'

Mum (laughing, normal accent): 'Shut up!'
Charlie: 'Peekoo!'

It also annoyed me that Mum hadn't told me that she was going out with Stephen. She had just told me that she was going out. She obviously didn't want me to know that it was with Stephen. Not until the actual night anyway. Maybe she didn't want to make a big deal out of it. Maybe she didn't want me to think that it was a big deal, she didn't want me to think that it was a big enough deal that she had to tell me about it before-hand. But she still wanted me to know. Why else would she have had Stephen pick her up? Or come into the house? Or think about having a drink with him then, in the house, before they went out?

All of this was whirring around in my head as I lay there, my head on Granny's chest.

But it was a big deal. It was a date. It wasn't just a happen-to-bump-into-each-other-and-have-a-drink thing. It was an arranged meeting between a man and a woman. Two grown-ups. That's a date if you ask me. And Stephen picking Mum up, in the evening, all dressed up.

And it was with Stephen. My football manager, Tina's dad. As deals go, they don't get much bigger.

I was sad, it seemed that I was always sad, but I was

also angry. I knew that I was angry at Mum, but I wasn't really sure why. Maybe it was because she was going on a date. Maybe it was because it was with Stephen. Maybe it was because she hadn't told me. Maybe it was because she was being annoying and showy-offy.

Maybe it was because it appeared that she was happy. Without Daddy. Maybe it was because she wasn't allowed to be happy.

'You're okay, love,' Granny said.

I noticed that I had stopped sobbing. I took my head away from Granny's chest.

'Sorry about your cardigan, Granny,' I said.

'Don't worry love,' said Granny. 'It needed a wash anyway. It hasn't been washed since August.'

She laughed. I smiled.

'I think I'm angry at Mum,' I said.

'I know, love,' said Granny. 'It's hard for you. I know how much you loved your dad. But your mum loved your dad too. As much as you did.'

I doubted it. Nobody loved Daddy as much as I loved Daddy.

'You're all dealing with it in different ways,' Granny continued. 'You're back playing football now, which is great. You're brilliant at football. Your mum is back working. That's great for her. She needed to go back to work. Life goes on. It doesn't mean that you think any less of your dad, or remember him any less fondly, but you have to get on with your lives too.'

That's the part that I was finding difficult.

'Do you think your dad would have wanted you to sit around moping all day?' Granny asked. 'Do you think he would have wanted you not to play football again? Do you think that he would have wanted you to do nothing else, just to think of him?'

'Of course he wouldn't,' I retorted. 'That's not the type of person he is.'

I stopped quickly. I had to stop quickly.

'That's not the type of person he was.'

I choked back some more tears so that I could continue to speak.

'I just think sometimes that I *shouldn't* be enjoying myself. Not without Daddy. I feel sometimes as if I shouldn't be happy, that I should be sad. That I need to be sad. That I need to remember to be sad. And if I am doing other things, I am not remembering Daddy. And I want to remember Daddy. All the time. Sometimes I'm afraid that I will forget him.'

Tears were streaming down my cheeks, but I was still able to speak.

Granny put her left hand up to my right cheek and

rubbed some of the tears away with her thumb. Her thumb was rough, but I liked the feeling. I felt comforted.

'You will always remember your daddy,' said Granny. 'He will always be your daddy and you will always be his daughter. No matter what. You will never forget him. And you know that he is looking down on you. He will never forget you.'

'What about Mum?' I blurted out.

Granny looked at me, lovingly, caringly.

'I can't have another dad, but she can have another husband. I'm not saying she's going to marry Stephen or anything, but she is out with him, on a date. Having fun. With someone else who isn't Daddy.'

Granny rubbed my cheek again, this time with the whole palm of her hand.

'Stephen is an old friend of your mum's,' said Granny. 'Stephen would spend as much time in this house when he was a young fellow as he did in his own house. Your mum needs her friends. And they're just going out for a drink. Just old friends having a drink together. That's all.'

I put my head back on Granny's chest again. Things seemed better. It felt good just to speak about it. I had never before spoken about my fear of forgetting Daddy.

I hadn't even really formed the thought in my head. It felt good to tell Granny about it, and for Granny to understand.

And maybe Mum going out with Stephen wasn't such a bad thing.

Just old friends having a drink.

I could feel the wool from Granny's cardigan against my cheek again, but I didn't mind the coarseness of it. My eyes were tingling, but I had stopped crying, and I didn't feel like crying any more. Actually, I felt like sleeping.

I heard Grandad coming into the room and asking if I was okay, and saying something about turning on the news, and I remember hearing the hum of the television, and I remember Granny telling me that I should go to bed, and I remember climbing the stairs on all fours with Granny behind me. But I don't remember brushing my teeth or actually getting into bed or Granny sitting on my bed for a little while, or hearing Mum coming home, or feeling her stroke my hair with her hand and telling me that it would get easier with time.

Chapter 17

• • • • • • •

EVENTFUL WEEK

I quite liked Irish and I quite liked Miss Donnelly. She was nice and I thought that she was a good Irish teacher.

'*Chonaic mé*,' said Miss Donnelly.

'I see,' said Aoife.

'*Go maith*,' said Miss Donnelly. 'And, I didn't see?' she asked.

A few hands went up.

'Rebecca,' said Miss Donnelly.

'*Níor chonaic mé*,' said Rebecca.

'*Ní hea*,' said Miss Donnelly. 'It's irregular, remember?'

More hands went up.

'Nuala.'

'*Ní fhaca mé*,' said Nuala.

'*Go maith*,' said Miss Donnelly. '*Go hiontach. Ní fhaca mé*. I didn't see.'

Some people wrote it down. Others didn't. I knew it, but I wrote it down anyway.

'*Chuala mé*,' said Miss Donnelly.

Did I hear?

Another show of hands.

'Rebecca.'

She did that, Miss Donnelly. She always gave you a chance to redeem yourself.

'*Ar chuala mé*,' said Rebecca, uncertainly. As if she was asking a question.

'*Go díreach!*' said Miss Donnelly, apparently genuinely happy that Rebecca had got it right. '*Maith thú*, Rebecca.'

'*Dúirt mé*,' said Miss Donnelly.

'I said,' said Robyn.

'*Go hiontach*,' said Miss Donnelly. 'Did you say?'

More hands.

'Ciara.'

Ciara hadn't had her hand up.

'*Ar dhúirt tú*.' Said Ciara, unconvincingly.

'*Ní hea*,' said Miss Donnelly with a sad expression on

her face, as if she was apologising for the fact that Ciara had got it wrong.

'Anna.'

I did have my hand up.

'*An ndúirt tú,*' I said.

'*Go maith,*' said Miss Donnelly. '*Maith thú, Anna.*'

The morning went quite quickly, which was good. I was glad when lunch time rolled around. I was quite hungry.

Training that evening was good too. It was great. The best ever I'd say. I wore my orange socks, and I played great. I probably played better than I had ever played in training for Ballymarra. Not only that, but I felt comfortable going in, I felt at ease with the girls, and I partnered with Debbie for the passing drills.

Debbie was lovely. We talked about lots of stuff, football, school, hair, socks.

'I like your orange socks,' she said.

'Yeah,' I said. 'Thanks.'

What else could I say? I wasn't going to say, yeah, my dad gave them to me on the morning that he died. I wanted to tell her about Daddy, but it wasn't appropriate. Not at training when we were supposed to be passing and listening, not talking.

'They're my favourite socks.'

146

Debbie was very good. Her passing was strong and accurate. Left foot or right foot, it didn't matter. She landed the ball on my chest almost every time. Side-foot or straight on. My passing was fairly good too. A few of my left-footed passes were a little weak, but overall I did well.

'Less talking there girls and more passing,' Patrick shouted at us once.

Debbie laughed.

'You're very good,' I said to Debbie as we got a drink of water while Patrick was passing out the bibs, everybody getting set for the game that would end the training session. 'Your passing is very accurate.'

'Thanks,' said Debbie quietly. 'So's yours.'

Well, what else could she say?

Patrick gave me an orange bib and I looked around to see who was on my team. Robyn had an orange bib, Rebecca had a blue one. Patrick usually split Robyn and Rebecca up. Debbie had an orange bib. Sinéad had an orange bib. It was looking like we had a lot of the strong players. Tina had a blue bib and she didn't look happy.

'These teams are not fair,' Tina was saying. 'Patrick, seriously. You have put Aoife and Rebecca on my team. They shouldn't be on the same team. They are two of the weakest players. Sorry girls, but you are.'

Everybody could hear Tina as she ploughed on, fil-terless.

'One of them should be with the oranges. And Debbie and Lily are on the same team. You should split them up. Put one of them on my team. Here, swap Debbie with Aoife.'

Tina tried to grab Aoife's blue bib as she was in the process of putting it on.

'Tina, stop,' said Patrick. 'That's enough out of you now. The teams are as they are. Get into your positions.'

Debbie and I laughed as we moved to get into our positions, up front. I had a quick look towards the space beyond the goals, but there was nothing there. No shadow. Of course there was no shadow. I was being ridiculous.

Daddy rarely went to training sessions anyway. Only to matches.

Then I kicked myself and told myself to cop myself on. For how long more would I go on looking for a shadow behind the goals? I hadn't seen it since that game against Croughton. Actually, that was the only time that I had seen it. And I wasn't sure that I had seen anything then either. The more time was moving on, the more I was thinking that I hadn't seen anything at all. That I had just imagined it. That I had seen what I had wanted to see.

'Do you want to go on the left or the right?' Debbie asked.

Debbie was looking at me as I came out of my daze, from my immersion in my mental ramblings. It took me a second or two to tune back into reality.

'I don't mind Debbie,' I said hesitantly. 'You're left-footed, right? You want to go on the right?'

'Sure we'll start like that then will we?' she said. 'Me on the right, you on the left. See how it goes.'

It went well. I played great. I got loads of the ball and I passed lots and I scored a goal and two points. Debbie played really well too. We linked up well together. We switched positions a couple of times. We didn't arrange it, it was just the way it happened. I ended up on the right a couple of times, and Debbie ended up on the left.

It didn't really matter to Debbie, she scored at least two points with her right foot from the left. It was a little awkward for me when I was on the right. It can be difficult for a right-footed player, playing on the right, but I figured it out. I scored a point from that side. You just had to start the ball out a little bit to the right of the goals and curl it in. And I enjoyed cutting inside and looking to give the pass. The game only lasted about twenty or twenty-five minutes, but I really enjoyed it.

Tina was awful. She wasn't chasing it at all. She started the game off giving out, and she ended it giving out, with lots of giving out in between. She gave out to her teammates, she gave out to Aoife for clearing the ball when she should have passed to her, and she gave out to Rebecca for passing to Edel when she should have cleared it. She even gave out to Edel once for passing to her. She somehow managed to argue that it was because of Edel's bad pass that she herself had kicked it wide. (Of course, it wasn't Tina's fault that she had kicked it wide.)

She gave out to herself once for missing. She must have forgotten herself for a second.

I was buzzing coming off the pitch, talking with Debbie and Lily and Robyn. It appeared that everyone had really enjoyed the game. Everyone on the orange team anyway. Then I saw Stephen, and my heart did a little flip. And not in a good way. It was my first time to see him since he had left our house in his tweed jacket with Mum. He looked more comfortable in his tracksuit.

'Well done girls,' he said. 'I only saw the last ten minutes or so of the game, but it looked great. Well played.'

'Thanks Stephen,' we all kind of said together.

'Debbie and Anna,' he said. 'Hold on there for a second.'

Debbie and I stopped. I wasn't worried. It wasn't about Mum, it wasn't about Sunday night, because he asked Debbie to stop as well. And it wasn't to give out to us because we had played badly, because we hadn't.

'I was watching the way that the two of you played together there,' said Stephen. 'It was very good. The way that you linked up. The way that you switched positions, naturally, as the play flowed, without the need for Patrick to call it. You complemented each other well. You filled in for each other when we were defending, and you helped each other when we were going forward.'

I didn't say anything. I didn't know what to say.

'Yeah it felt good,' Debbie said.

'Thanks,' I said.

Thanks? Really?!

'We might try that in the semi-final next week,' Stephen continued. 'Play one of you on the right and one of you on the left, but give both of you free roles. Leave it up to the two of you to switch when you want, when you think it's right. If you can do that, without me or Patrick calling it from the sideline, it could work very well. It would confuse the hell out of their defenders, that's for sure. Pull them out of position. What do you think?'

'I'd be happy to give it a go,' said Debbie.

'Anna?'

This was great. Great that Stephen had seen us play, great that he thought that we were good, great that he was thinking about this tactic, which would mean that I would be starting in the semi-final, and that I would be starting at left half-forward or right half-forward.

'Are you as happy playing on the right as you are on the left?' asked Stephen.

I tried to be cool.

'Yeah, like Debbie,' I said. 'I'd be happy to give it a go. I've never really played on the right before, but I quite liked it there. I liked shooting from the right, I think I'm figuring it out, and I liked cutting in from the right side. I know that was only a training game, but it could work well in a real game.'

'Okay, great,' said Stephen, and he walked over to Patrick.

'That's good isn't it?' said Debbie as we walked towards the gate.

'Yeah,' I said hesitantly. 'I think so. I hope that I'll know what to do.'

'I hope I will too!' said Debbie. 'But it worked well there. There's no reason why it can't work in a real game. We can figure it out.'

'Debbie!'

It was Tina, standing beside the dressing room door.

'Come here for a second, will you Debs?'

Debbie looked annoyed.

'What's up Tina?'

'Just come here for a second,' said Tina again. Sinéad and Edel were with her, all three still in their football gear.

Debbie looked at me apologetically.

'Okay, see you Debbie,' I said. 'My mum is probably waiting for me anyway. See you later.'

I broke into a jog and headed off towards the car park. Debbie said bye. Bye, Anna. I didn't know why Tina wanted Debbie. I suspected that she only wanted Debbie because Debbie was talking to me. It didn't really matter anyway. I didn't care. And I was right, Mum was waiting for me.

It was unusual to see Mum's car in the car park after training without Stephen's head beside the open driver's window. Mum had the radio on and the windows up when I got into the car.

'Hi, pet,' she said. 'How was training?'

'It was great, Mum,' I said.

Mum lit up.

I told her everything on the way home. About how well I played, about how well I got on with Debbie, about how we switched positions, about what Stephen had said to us afterwards, about what that all meant, that I would probably be starting in the semi-final. And not in the corner. That I would probably be starting left half-forward or right half-forward.

Mum can sometimes look a bit dazed when I go on for too long about football, she can glaze over when I go into too much detail, but she looked completely interested in all this, so I kept talking. The more detail I went into, the more interested she appeared to be, so the more detail I went into. She seemed to be really interested in all of it.

Then I told her about Tina. I didn't tell her about the incident at lunch time, but I told her about Tina calling Debbie over to her at the end of training, just because I was talking to Debbie, it seemed.

'That was a bit odd wasn't it?' Mum said.

I was glad she thought so too.

Chapter 18

MINEFIELD

We had an hour to play Minecraft.

'Mum, can me and Charlie play Minecraft?'

'Can who play Minecraft?'

'Me and Charlie.'

'*Who?*'

'Ah Mum. Can *Charlie and I* play Minecraft?

Pyjamas at nine, lights out at half-nine, that was the deal. That gave us just over an hour. We joined worlds, me on Mum's iPad, Charlie on her phone, and in Creative mode. Charlie liked to play in Creative mode. He liked that he had all his stuff from the start, that he didn't have to build up his inventory. That he didn't have to cut down trees or make wood or find iron to make his tools. And he liked that he could fly, and that he couldn't die.

Mainly, though, Charlie was scared of the monsters in Survival mode. There were no monsters in Creative.

Being honest, I always preferred Creative mode too. I used Charlie as an excuse, as my reason for playing in Creative mode, but actually, it made things a lot easier. You could get things done a lot more quickly.

I had been building Croke Park for a while. I had laid the pitch and I had put up the goals and I was building the stadium around the pitch. The Hogan Stand and the Cusack Stand and Hill 16. And the dressing rooms. I didn't know what the dressing rooms in Croke Park were like, but my dressing rooms were fairly elaborate, with cushioned seats and headrests and television screens for video analysis.

Charlie was building a house out of dirt beside the stadium, behind Hill 16. Where Clonliffe Road should have been. Maybe he was planning to live on Clonliffe Road, so that he could be close to Croke Park.

I had almost finished building my stadium when Mum said bedtime. I just had to finish off the Davin Stand at the Canal End and put the roof on. Charlie had just about finished the walls of his house.

'But I just want to put on my roof,' Charlie said in that irritating and irritated voice of his that annoys everybody.

'It's after nine, Charlie,' said Mum, in her stern no-room-for-negotiation voice.

Tears.

I had put on my pyjamas and was brushing my teeth when I heard Mum speaking on the phone on the landing, just outside the slightly open bathroom door. I thought I heard her say Brenda. Was she on the phone to Brenda? Sally's mum? I hadn't spoken to Sally in ages. I stopped brushing my teeth. Toothbrush still in mouth, hand still on toothbrush.

'It's not like the last time, Brenda,' Mum was saying. 'We're not kids any more.'

The toothpaste was stinging my mouth. I never liked that extra minty toothpaste that Mum always got.

'We were young the last time,' Mum was saying. 'And it was fun. And we both knew about college. It's different now. We're grown up. Everything is more serious.'

I couldn't bear the stinging in my mouth any longer. I had to spit. I turned the tap on fully and doused my lips, my mouth, almost my whole face.

What was that all about?

157

I filled my mouth up with water and spat. What was fun? What's different now? Why is it different now? I filled my mouth up with water again, and spat again. And again. Relief.

By the time I had come back up for air again, Mum was standing beside me in the bathroom. She still had her phone in her hand, but it looked like Brenda had gone.

She looked at me, a bit sheepishly. I didn't know what to say to her, and it looked like she didn't know what to say to me. She spoke first.

'Are you finished, pet?'

'I am,' I said, as I put my toothbrush back into the cup.

'Okay come on then,' she said. 'Bed. It's nearly half-nine.'

I walked out of the bathroom, past Mum, into my room. It was all a little awkward. I pulled back the covers and got into bed. Mum followed me into my room.

'Are you okay, pet?'

'Yes,' I said.

'Okay,' said Mum. 'I'll just go into Charlie. I'll be back to tuck you in.'

I never understood that one. Tuck you in. I didn't

need to be tucked in. What does tuck you in mean anyway? My duvet was never tucked in.

I could hear Mum talking to Charlie in his room across the landing and through the open doors. He was still going on about the roof on his house. What if it rained during the night? Mum wasn't sure if it rained in Minecraft. Charlie assured her that it did.

I turned off my light and allowed my head fall heavily onto my pillow.

Mum said that it probably wouldn't rain in Minecraft if Charlie wasn't there to see it. Charlie said that it could. That lots of things happen in Minecraft even if you are not there. That monsters and villagers and zombies do all sorts of things. Mum reasoned that they could worry about it in the morning. Charlie didn't seem to be too convinced, but he seemed to realise that argument was futile. That he was in bed and that he was going to sleep.

I closed my eyes when I heard Mum coming towards my room. I could sense the room darken as she walked in, momentarily blocking the light that was coming in from the landing. I could feel her sit on my bed and I could feel her hand as it gently touched my back.

'Are you okay, pet?' she asked again.

'Yes,' I said again, sleepily this time. 'Just tired.'

'Okay,' said Mum. 'See you in the morning then.'

She kissed me on the head.

'Night, pet,' she said.

'Night, Mum.'

In truth, I wasn't tired. Not at all. My head was racing. Mum obviously hadn't wanted me to hear the conversation that she had had with Brenda. She was embarrassed by it. They were young last time. Who? They're grown-ups now. Who are grown-ups now? Brenda and Mum? An old boyfriend of Brenda's? An old boyfriend of Mum's?

Things are different now. What things? Things are more serious. How? They were kids then. They both knew something about college. They both knew what? That they were going to college? But Mum met Brenda in college. Didn't she? There was something about an end to it. What about an end to it, and an end to what?

I eventually fell asleep with all of this running through my head. It was still there when I got up the following morning. Was Mum talking about a boyfriend she had before she met Daddy?

I was probably quieter than usual in the car with Mum on the way to school.

'What's wrong, pet?' she asked me eventually.

'Nothing, Mum,' I lied. 'Really. Nothing more than

the usual stuff.'

'Is this about my conversation with Brenda last night?'

'No.'

'Is it?'

'No, Mum. Really. It isn't.'

Silence for a few minutes.

'I'll tell you what it was about pet if it's bothering you.'

'It isn't.'

Then I thought about it for a minute or two. This was ridiculous. Mum said that she would tell me about it if it was bothering me, and it was bothering me.

'Okay, it is,' I said. Now it was my turn to be sheepish.

'Okay,' said Mum.

'So what was it about?' I asked. 'You said that you would tell me.'

'I did,' said Mum. 'And I will.'

I looked at her. She glanced at me quickly as she drove. Eyes on the road, eyes on me momentarily, eyes back on the road. That's a good trick, I thought. If you have something difficult to say to somebody, you should tell them while you are driving. It means that you don't have to look them in the eye.

'Okay,' said Mum.

She paused and took a breath.

'Stephen and I ...'

She paused again.

Stephen? Really?

'We used to be kind of boyfriend and girlfriend. Years ago. When I was here. At home. When I lived here. Before I went to college. Before I went to Galway. Before I met Dad.'

I felt weak. I hadn't seen that one coming. Stephen and Mum? As teenagers? In school? Boyfriend and girlfriend? I was flabbergasted. I looked at Mum and exclaimed something. Something like, really? Or, seriously? Or, are you joking? Mum continued as if I hadn't said anything.

'It wasn't serious,' she said. 'We were just kids. We just hung out together here, with our friends. There was a group of us, and Stephen and I were just in that group. We'd hang out in the village or go to the cinema or go to someone's house. We just got on well together.'

I just stared straight ahead of me at the road. There was a little spot on the windscreen in front of me, and if I moved my head, I could make it move its position on the road. I could move it in and out between the white lines in the centre of the road, like a slalom.

'What do you think of that?' asked Mum anxiously.

I wasn't sure, so I told her that.

'I'm not sure,' I said.

Silence. Mum appeared to be happy to sit and drive in silence. She won. I broke the silence. I had too many questions.

'Why didn't you tell me this before?' I asked eventually.

'I didn't think that you needed to know.'

So she was only telling me things that she thought I needed to know? What else was she keeping from me?

'Were you not going to tell me at all?'

'I don't know,' said Mum. 'I hadn't really thought about whether I should tell you or not.'

'Was it not relevant?'

'I didn't think it was that important.'

'And yet, you tell Brenda?'

'Brenda knew,' said Mum. 'Brenda has always known. Brenda knows Stephen.'

More silence as my thoughts swirled. Mum and Stephen, boyfriend and girlfriend. In school, in college, hanging out with Brenda and probably her boyfriend. Going to parties and laughing and sitting in parks and having fun.

What about Daddy?

'And where was Daddy?' I asked suddenly, out loud.

'He was in school in Galway pet,' said Mum. 'I hadn't

met him at that stage. I didn't know him.' She looked at me softly. 'I was waiting to meet him.'

Daddy was probably studying, I thought. And playing football.

'So you wouldn't have told me if I hadn't overheard you telling Brenda?'

I had lots of questions, and I wasn't certain that I was going to be able to structure them into any kind of logical order. I decided that I would just ask them as they came to me.

'Not now anyway,' said Mum. 'I wasn't planning to tell you last night or this morning anyway.'

'So when were you planning to tell me?'

'I don't know, pet.'

'Oh, that's right,' I said. 'You weren't planning on telling me at all. You didn't think that I needed to know.'

Mum said nothing. She seemed hurt. I regretted that. That came out more harshly than I had intended. My tone was bad. Even so, I wasn't apologising for it. I couldn't. I didn't feel like apologising. I was the injured party here and the injured party doesn't apologise.

We arrived at the school drop-off zone and Mum stopped the car.

'Are you and Stephen boyfriend and girlfriend again?' I asked, teary-eyed.

'No!' said Mum emphatically.

'But you've been out together?'

'Just for a drink. Just once or twice.'

Once or twice?

'So, it wasn't serious then, but it is serious now?' I asked, my questions gathering pace.

'I didn't say that,' said Mum.

'So, is it?'

'Is it what?'

'Serious. Is it serious now?'

'No. Of course it isn't.'

'Then why did you tell Brenda that it was?'

'I didn't.'

'You did. You said that everything was more serious now.'

'Did I?'

'Yes Mum, you did.'

'Well, it is I suppose. Everything is more serious. I have you and Charlie. I have responsibilities. It's not just me anymore.'

'So then, you need a husband?'

'What?!'

'You have me and Charlie. So you need a husband?'

'No, I don't need a husband. That's crazy. I just mean that I have to think carefully about everything now.'

'Like about Stephen?'

'No. Not about Stephen. Well, not just about Stephen. About everything. I can't just allow things happen any more without thinking about them, without thinking them through. Without thinking of the possible conse- quences. I need to think about what's best for you and Charlie and me.'

I had to get out of the car. You weren't allowed stay in the drop-off zone for longer than it took to drop your kid off. If you did, the other parents would start to get angry. They'd start to beep at you and everything. Nobody had beeped at us yet, but I still sensed that I had to get out. I opened the car door.

Mum grabbed my arm gently but firmly.

'Are you okay, pet?'

I nodded my head.

'I don't want you going off to school upset,' said Mum. 'It's not a big deal. Really. We can talk about it later again though.'

'I'm fine, Mum,' I said.

'I have to work a little late this evening,' said Mum, 'but I'll be home before bedtime, so we can talk about it again then.'

I just nodded. She leaned over and kissed me on the cheek.

'Have a good day in school.'

I didn't have a good day in school. Not really. It was fine, but it was long. No PE, and double science with Ms McHugh in the afternoon always made the day seem longer than it needed to be. And all those thoughts about Mum marrying Stephen were going around in my head again. It was unimaginable. Really.

I couldn't imagine sharing Mum with Stephen, or sharing a room or even a house with stupid Tina. And that was without even thinking about the biggest thing in all of this, about Stephen replacing Daddy.

Mum wasn't home when I got home from school, which always made me feel a little sad. Granny was there though, and she made me hot chocolate, which was always a nice consolation prize if Mum wasn't home. I had my hot chocolate at the kitchen table as I did my homework.

Sally didn't call. Sally rarely called during the week. Charlie was in his room, or in the sitting room watching television, or playing with razor blades somewhere. I didn't really know. I presumed that Granny knew where he was.

My homework took a while. I had a lot. My history essay, in particular, took a long time. Did it really matter that they lived in huts made of wattle and daub back about twelve thousand years ago?

I was in my pyjamas and watching television with Granny and Grandad and Charlie when Mum came home.

'Mummy!'

Charlie sprang up off the floor and ran out of the sitting room and into the hall as soon as he heard the front door opening. It's so cute. He loves his Mummy more than he loves anything else in the world. Even more than he loves that little beat-up bunny that he brings to bed with him, who has only one ear and no eyes. Bunny, he calls it.

I waited until Mum came into the sitting room with Charlie in her arms before I got up and went over to her.

'Hi pet,' she said. 'How was your day?'

'Fine,' I said.

No lie there. I gave Mum a hug, which meant that I had to kind of give a hug too to Charlie, who was still attached to Mum.

'Hi Mum, Dad,' said Mum. 'Everything okay?'

'Everything is just great love,' said Granny as she got up. 'Sit down there, I'll get you a cup of tea.'

'You know what,' said Mum. 'I'll have one afterwards. I think I'd better get these two to bed first. Especially this one!'

She started to squeeze Charlie's leg so that he wriggled and laughed and eventually dropped to the floor.

'Come on you two. Upstairs.'

I was in bed and reading my book when Mum came in.

'Charlie is almost asleep there, standing up, brushing his teeth!' she said. 'He's wrecked.'

I smiled.

'So did you think any more about what we were talking about this morning?' Mum asked.

'Not really,' I lied.

Mum looked surprised, and a little disappointed.

'Oh.'

She leaned against the open door.

'Okay,' she said.

Awkward silence as I contemplated how to break it.

'Well, actually,' I said, 'a little.'

When the answer really was a lot. An awful lot.

'Right,' said Mum.

'And?'

'And what?' I asked.

I knew that I wasn't being fair on Mum. I was bursting to ask her hundreds of questions, and I knew that she was wanting to answer them, but I still wanted to play it coolly. I hadn't seen her all day. It took me time to warm up.

'And do you have any more questions?' asked Mum.

'A few,' I said.

'Riiiigghhhht,' she said slowly.

'Don't you want to put Charlie to bed first?' I asked.

'Charlie's fine,' said Mum, a little sternly. 'Now, what do you want to know?'

'Lots of things,' I said, a little more enthusiastically than I had intended.

'Like what?'

'Like, did you want to marry Stephen?'

I blurted it out.

'Ah pet,' said Mum, as she sat down carefully on my bed beside me. 'I didn't want to marry anyone then. I was only a few years older than you are now. And how far from your thoughts is marriage? All I was thinking about was having fun, and leaving school, and going to college, and how excited I was about that.'

'And did Stephen not go to college?'

'No he didn't. He was always staying here.'

'Did he not want to go with you to college?'

'We never really discussed it, pet,' said Mum. 'He was never going. He was always going to work with his dad here. He was never going to leave Ballymarra.'

That made sense to me. Stephen knew everyone in Ballymarra.

'And were you sad leaving him?' I asked.

'A little,' said Mum. 'But only a little. Really. I was more excited about going to college, about going to Galway, than I was sad about leaving anybody.'

'And did you stay boyfriend and girlfriend when you were in Galway?'

The questions were tumbling out of me now.

'No we didn't. I think that Stephen wanted to, but it didn't make sense. We were at different ends of the country. I left in September and I was probably only going to get home once before Christmas.'

I found it difficult to imagine, Mum and Stephen, boyfriend and girlfriend. I didn't like it. Even when he called around to pick her up for that date, which wasn't a date, I didn't like it, but it didn't seem like they were boyfriend and girlfriend. It was just like they were hanging out together, like people who knew each other, that he was giving her a lift. Not that they were going out together.

I couldn't imagine Mum kissing anybody but Daddy. They belonged together, and neither of them belonged to anyone else. Mum now without Daddy was difficult enough. But seeing her with another man who wasn't

Daddy. That would just be impossible to ever imagine or to ever get used to.

'Did you love Stephen?'

Mum stopped for a second. I wasn't sure if she was going to smile or cry, or smile *and* cry. I regretted asking the question. I wasn't sure whether or not she wanted to tell me the answer, and I wasn't sure that I wanted to know the answer anyway. If I could have rewound then, I would have rewound and erased the question.

'I was young,' Mum said carefully. 'I didn't know what love was. I thought at one point that maybe I did love Stephen. But, actually, I know now that I didn't. Not really.'

She looked at me softly and pushed the hair that had fallen down on the left-hand side of my face back behind my ear.

'I liked the idea of being in love I think,' she said. 'But I wasn't in love.'

That was a relief. I didn't want her to love anyone before she had loved Daddy, or to love anyone else ever. Only Daddy. I had the answer that I wanted. Even so, I needed to be sure.

'Did you love him as much as you loved Daddy?'

I could feel the tears coming before I had finished the sentence.

Mum put her arms behind my back and pulled me towards her, so that I was sitting up in my bed with my head against her shoulder blade and my right ear against her left ear.

'Pet, I never loved anyone as much as I loved Daddy,' she said. 'As much as I love Daddy. I couldn't possibly. Nobody ever loved anyone as much as I love Daddy or as much as he loved me. I love Daddy more than you can imagine. More than anyone can imagine. It was when I met Daddy that I realised that I hadn't loved Stephen at all. Not even close.'

Mum's voice was quivering now.

'And when I met Daddy that was it for me. College, friends, sport, career, nothing was more important to me than him, and then you and Charlie. The four of us together. And nothing was more important to him than the three of us. And I knew as soon as I met Daddy that I wanted to spend the rest of my life with him.'

Now Mum was crying.

'Or at least the rest of his life.'

We just stayed there for a few minutes, arms in arms, me sitting up in my bed, she sitting on the side of my bed, her arms around me, my head buried in her shoulder. She was warm and my face was wet and her top was wet. I think that we were both trying to stop crying.

'Everybody okay in there?'

Granny was knocking on the door and opening it at the same time, and poking her head in. Mum relaxed the grip that she had on me and turned her head to look at Granny. She smiled and nodded. Granny smiled back.

'Because there's a little man here who wants to say goodnight.'

Charlie bounced into the room in the Spider Man pyjamas that hugged his little frame like a leotard. Wrecked indeed! He jumped on top of my bed beside Mum, knelt up high and stretched his arms skywards in triumph:

'I've finished my roof!'

• • • • • •

Chapter 19

SEMI-EXCITED

I was nervous when I woke up on Sunday morning. I went to bed nervous on Saturday night, I slept nervous, and I got up nervous.

It was good nervous though. Excited nervous. It was nervous like, nervous before an exam when you have studied well for it. Or before you meet Ariana Grande. (Not that I have ever met Ariana Grande, but I imagine that I would be excited-nervous if I was about to.) Not nervous like you would be if you were about to meet Pennywise the Dancing Clown.

It was an exciting day. Semi-final day. And I would be starting, probably on the left wing, left half-forward, with Debbie on the right, and switching with her. I was looking forward to that lots. I was looking forward to playing with Debbie, each of us as wing forward, and switching with her as we had been practicing in training. I was looking forward to seeing if we could be as good in a semi-final, against real opponents, against Ardart, as we had been in training.

I didn't know much about Ardart. They were from the other side of the county and I had never played against them. The girls were saying that they were tough though. That their players were tough and that their coaches were tough, and that we had to be tough back. Edel had broken her arm in a tackle in an Under-11 game against them three years ago. It was an accident apparently, but the Ardart girls hadn't been very apologetic about it. Rebecca told me that Edel had been one of the best players on the team before that incident, and that she hadn't been the same player since.

I was sitting up in my bed when Mum opened by bedroom door.

'Morning pet,' she smiled.

'Hi Mum.'

'What's going on today?' Mum asked. 'Anything extraordinary?'

For a second I thought that she was serious. Or for

less than a second. Half a second. Maybe even less than that.

'Mum!'

She sat on my bed and hugged me.

'You'll be great,' she said. 'I know you will.'

I didn't know that I would be. I was nervous. But I felt good. I was playing well in training, I was getting on well with most of the girls, and I was developing a good understanding with Debbie on the pitch. She was a selfless player, she always looked to pass to a player who was in a better position. I loved playing with that type of player. I thought and hoped that I was that type of player.

It was taking time but, slowly, the girls were starting to accept me as part of the team. I was still the new girl, but I felt that I was becoming less and less the new girl as time was moving on, and more and more just a normal member of the team. A good member of the team. An important member of the team I hoped.

I got up, had a shower, and started to get my gear out. Black shorts, green socks. Under armour. Tracksuit top. Gum shield. I might need my gum shield all right, if the girls were right about the Ardart girls.

I opened my bottom drawer and took out my orange socks. I couldn't wear my orange socks. I couldn't be the only one wearing orange socks, with all the other girls wearing the club's green socks. It was a semi-final. I wouldn't be allowed even if I wanted to. Or I couldn't wear my orange socks on the outside.

I put on my shorts and my training top. Then I took one of my orange socks, and carefully put it on my left foot, stretching it over my foot and up to my knee, before folding it down so that the top of the sock was just below my knee-cap. I did the same with the other orange sock, stretched it up to my right knee, then tucked it down. Then I took one of my green socks, and stretched it over my orange sock on my left foot. Stretched it up my leg, up above my knee, then tucked it down so that the top of the sock sat just below my knee-cap, but just above the top of my orange sock. I did the same with my right foot. Stretched the green sock up over my orange sock, up to my knee, then turned it down.

I stood up. Two pairs of socks. My feet felt a little fat. I stood up on my tip-toes, and down again. Up on my tip-toes, and down again. I bounced around like that for a few seconds. Then I jumped up a few inches in the air, with my legs straight, just using my ankles as leverage, and landed softly on my tip-toes. I did that again. It felt fine. It didn't feel like my feet were stuffed with cotton wool.

I got the smell of the grill from the kitchen before I got to the bottom of the stairs.

'An elite athlete needs a good breakfast!' said Mum from over at the cooker as I walked into the kitchen. Granny and Grandad were already there, sitting at the table, empty plates in front of them, drinking tea. Charlie was on the floor with about 17 thousand little plastic figures around him.

I gave Granny a kiss, then went over to Grandad and gave him a kiss too.

'Are you all set love?' asked Granny.

'I think so,' I said.

☣ ☣ ☣

I must have been the last to arrive at the Killinvagh pitch – neutral venue for the semi-final – because the girls started to file into the dressing room just as I was walking from Mum's car towards them. People found their places in the dressing room. Different dressing room, but the usual places. Broadly.

I found a space between Robyn and Amanda.

'Hi Robyn,' I said. 'Hi Amanda. Rebecca.'

The girls nodded and muttered something. Hi, probably. Hi Anna.

There was a strange atmosphere in the dressing room. There was a strange silence. A nervous silence. An eerie hum. In all my time with Ballymarra, I had never known Tina to be quiet before a match or a training session. But she was. I had to look over to 'her' corner to make sure that she was there. And she was. Sinéad on her left, Edel on her right. The usual.

Debbie was opposite me, beside Lily. I caught her eye and smiled. She smiled back. All set.

There was a knock on the door and Orla's mum came in.

'Everybody ready?' she asked. 'Everybody okay?'

Hums and nods and murmurings. She opened the door and went back out, holding the door open for Stephen and Patrick as she left.

Stephen and Patrick both looked concerned. Concentrating. Nervous.

'Okay girls,' said Stephen quietly, and even the nervous hum became quiet. There wasn't a sound, not even a mutter or a throat-clear before Stephen spoke again.

'We have made some changes to the team for today,' he said.

Maybe I was playing on the right, and Debbie on the left. Maybe he would start us off like that, see how we would go. I didn't mind. The right was not my natural side, as a right-footer, whereas, as a left-footer, it was Debbie's, but I was happy to start off there. See how it would go. And we would be switching anyway.

'Some people might be disappointed that they are not starting,' continued Stephen.

Maybe he wasn't going to start Shelley, the usual left half-forward. That wouldn't be good though. Shelley was a good player. Better to push Shelley to left full-forward and not start Aoife or Ciara.

'But don't worry,' said Stephen. 'The subs are just as important as the first fifteen.'

That's not true, I thought to myself.

'Some of the subs will be coming on, for sure,' said Stephen. 'And remember, this is a team. This is our team. All twenty-two, not just the first fifteen.'

I glanced over at Debbie. She was just looking at the ground, at her feet on the ground. I looked down at my feet as Stephen started to name the team.

'Sofia,' he called, as the goalkeeper's jersey flew through the air.

'Just get ready now and we'll talk about it out there after we've named the team.'

Sofia grabbed the jersey and started to put it on over her under armour. Even Sofia wasn't up to her usual goalkeeper's antics.

'Rebecca, right corner-back,' said Stephen as he threw the number two jersey to Rebecca.

'Robyn, full-back.'

Number three.

'Edel, left corner.'

Number four.

Robyn and Rebecca started to put on their jerseys beside me.

'Lily, midfield,' said Stephen, as he threw the number eight jersey to Lily.

'Shelley,' he said, as he threw her a jersey. It looked like the number nine jersey. Tina's jersey.

'We're going to try you in midfield today,' said Stephen. Shelley grabbed the jersey and looked at Stephen. She looked puzzled. Frightened even. 'We'll have a chat about it in a second,' said Stephen. 'Don't worry about it. You're well able for midfield. You know you are.'

At once, I felt sorry for Shelley and sorry for Tina. Shelley was being thrown into a position for which she wasn't prepared, in which she had little or no experience as far as I knew, and she was taking Tina's place there. No wonder Tina had been so quiet. I looked over at Tina, but she was just looking down at the ground, hair down over her ears so that I couldn't see her face.

Was she injured? Was she devastated?

'Number 10,' Stephen said as his eyes darted around the room. My heart rose a little in expectation.

'Debbie,' said Stephen, as his eyes alighted on Debbie, and he threw her jersey to her.

Fair enough, I thought. I wasn't starting right half-forward. Left half-forward was fine. It was where I wanted to be anyway. It was where I wanted to start. Then I could switch with Debbie as the game progressed, as we had discussed with Stephen.

'Centre half-forward,' said Stephen as his eyes darted around the room again.

'Sinéad.'

He threw number 11 to Sinéad. Sinéad caught it with one hand. Expressionless. Unfazed.

'Left half-forward,' said Stephen.

I almost put my hand up.

'Tina,' he said.

Wait, what? Tina? Really?

I watched in wonder, my mouth half open, as Stephen threw the number 12 jersey over towards Tina in the far corner. It fell short, it landed on the floor beside Edel, so that Edel had to pick it up off the ground and hand it to Tina, who grabbed it quickly.

I couldn't believe it. I wasn't starting at left half-forward or right half-forward. What had happened to me and Debbie starting on the wings, one on each wing, and switching as the game progressed? What about the chat that Stephen had had with us? About how well it had worked in training and about how well it could work in a match?

Maybe Stephen had a different plan. Start me in the corner, left full-forward or right full-forward, and that Debbie and I could switch between the wing and the corner. Or maybe he was going to give me the number 13 or the number 15 jersey, so that Ardart would think that I was playing in the corner, and actually play me on the wing, and switch with Debbie. That would confuse Ardart even more. Hopefully it would confuse Ardart more than it would confuse us.

By the time I had consoled myself with this thought, Stephen had already given the number 13 jersey to Ciara and had called number 14, full-forward.

'Amanda,' he said, as he threw number 14 to Amanda.

'And left full-forward,' he said.

Suddenly, I had an awful thought. What if I wasn't number 15? I probably was, but what if I wasn't? There was only one place left on the starting 15 and I didn't have one yet. I did a quick scour of the room. Ciara was putting on number 13. Aoife was sitting there stony-faced, in her under armour. She didn't have a jersey yet either. It was between me and Aoife. I deserved the jersey more than Aoife. I was better than Aoife. Wasn't I?

'Aoife,' said Stephen.

Aoife's face lit up. I watched as she looked over at Stephen and as she caught the green jersey that he had thrown to her.

A pit opened in the bottom of my stomach. I felt weak. Nauseous. The room started spinning. Stephen was saying something about how important the subs were, but I didn't care. They weren't important. They weren't as important as the fifteen who were starting.

Why wasn't I starting? I thought that I was a good player. I didn't think that I was the best player on the team or anything, but I thought that I was good enough to start. I thought that I was in the best fifteen. And I thought that I was doing well in training. And I thought that Stephen thought that I was doing well in training.

'Here Anna.'

Stephen threw me a jersey. It didn't matter what number it was. There was a two on it, I could see as it flew through the air. Twenty something. I didn't catch it. I allowed it land on my knees. I just looked at Stephen, but he wasn't looking at me. I couldn't believe it.

A hum started up around the dressing room again. An excited hum. I wasn't excited. It was all I could do to stop myself from crying. I could feel Robyn looking at me.

'Are you not starting?' she asked.

I shook my head. I didn't dare to speak in case I would start crying.

'What the hell?' Robyn exclaimed. 'What the hell is that all about?'

I had no response. I didn't know the answer and I couldn't have answered, I couldn't have spoken, even if I had known the answer.

'You're one of our best players.'

Rebecca leaned over.

'What? Is Anna not starting?'

I just looked down at the ground, and continued to concentrate on not crying. It took all my energy. Imagine crying because you didn't make the starting fifteen? How big a baby would you be? How self-absorbed?

'No, she's not,' said Robyn.

'That's not right,' said Rebecca. 'That's a mistake. Does Stephen know?'

'Stephen decided it!' said Robyn. 'He gave her a sub's jersey.'

She picked up the jersey that was still on my knees

and held it up so that she could see the number.

'Number 21.'

Most of the girls were standing up now. The sound of football boots on tiled floor was getting more audible as more and more girls started to stand up and move their feet. All itching to get out there now.

'Okay,' said Stephen. 'Let's get out there and get a kick around, then we can have a chat about it.'

The girls filed out the door, in ones and twos, some of them almost tripping over others in their anxiousness to get out. I half-watched as they did. It was all a bit of a blur. Tina and Edel and Debbie and Amanda. All of them starting. Lily and Ciara and Sinéad and Aoife.

Robyn put her hand on my shoulder.

'Are you okay?'

I had gathered myself a little.

'Of course I'm okay,' I said. 'I'm not starting. So what? It's not a big deal. I might come on at some point.'

Robyn rubbed my shoulder. She knew that it was a big deal. And I knew that she knew that it was a big deal.

'You could be an impact sub!'

I laughed. Robyn laughed.

'I'll be fine,' I said. 'Thanks though.'

Robyn left. She was the last one out of the dressing

room. Or the second last one. I was last. I still didn't have my jersey on. I held it up in front of me. Number 21. Number 21 indeed. I still had to fight back the urge to cry. I couldn't go out onto the pitch with tears in my eyes.

I put on my jersey and my tracksuit top, and walked towards the door. As I did, Patrick arrived at the door from the outside with another man, probably somebody from Killinvagh. He had a big bunch of keys in his hand. It seemed like they were both surprised to see me, surprised that there was someone still in the dressing room.

'Come on,' Patrick said.

Not Anna. Not come on Anna. Just come on.

'We have to lock up.'

I walked out the door and past Patrick and the man with the keys. I was gone about five paces when Patrick called to me.

'Anna,' he said.

I stopped and looked back at him.

'Don't worry about it. You should have started. You'll be on soon.'

I smiled. That was nice of Patrick. Behind that tough exterior, his heart may not be that cold after all.

The girls were all warming up when I got to the

pitch. All twenty-one of them, in two groups, doing a hand-passing drill.

I had a look behind the goals. There was nobody there. Not that I expected anybody to be there. Not Daddy. I don't know why I looked. It just made me sad. Sadder than I was.

I missed Daddy more than ever. At times like these. Little setbacks. Not starting. If he had been there, he would have helped me to see the positive. I don't know what he would have said, but it would have been the right thing. It's probably just a tactical thing. Something like that. You know that you're good enough to start. Or, the manager hasn't seen your true capabilities yet. Or, it's great that you're good enough to be part of the panel. I don't know what it would have been, but it would have made me feel better. I tried to imagine what it would have been, but I couldn't, and I felt even worse because I couldn't.

'Come on Anna,' said Stephen. 'Join in here, in this group.'

It was the first thing that Stephen had said to me since he had given me the number 21 jersey. No explanation, no reason why I wasn't starting. I was re-assured by Robyn and by Rebecca though. And by Patrick. I wasn't the only one who thought that I should have been starting. I felt much better for that. But obviously Stephen didn't share that view, and his was really the only view that mattered.

I joined in the hand-passing drill. Catch, pass, move. Join the back of the line. Shuffle forward, shuffle forward, shuffle forward. Catch, pass, move. Join the back of the line. All fast, all sharp. I liked this drill, and I immersed myself in it.

'Okay, girls,' shouted Stephen. 'Kick passes now. Move back to the cones.'

I liked the kick passing drill too. From about ten yards, see if you could land the ball in your team mate's chest. Straight on, low and hard. Move, join the back of the line. Catch, kick, move. Join the back of the line. After about five minutes of that, Stephen called us into a huddle.

I joined the huddle, but I didn't really feel like I was part of it. A substitute. All that he was saying was for the starting fifteen. I heard bits of it, but only bits of it. Sofia, look for the short kick-out if it's on. If it's not on, hit it hard down the centre. Look for Lily or Shelley in the middle. Get the ball up to the half-forwards as quickly as you can. Get the ball to Debbie or Sinéad or Tina. Debbie, start on the right, Tina on the left, but feel free to switch wings when you want, as we have spoken about.

My heart sank into the pit of my stomach. That was our thing, Debbie's and mine. We had come up with it. We had worked it in training, and we had worked on it in training to try to perfect it. Now it looked like Debbie and Tina were going to be doing it. And I was a sub.

I wanted to break away from the huddle, but that would have been too obvious, so I stayed until Stephen had finished talking. Then it was over to Tina.

'Who are we?'

'Ballymarra!'

'Who are we?'

'Ballymarra!'

'Who are we?'

'Ballymarra! Ballymarra! Ballymarra!'

I didn't join in. I didn't have the voice. I didn't have the heart. I just wanted to go home but, given that going home was not an option, I just wanted to sit in the dug-out and wallow in self-pity.

I saw Mum on the sideline as I started to stroll over to the dug-out, just before I heard a soft voice behind me.

'Anna.'

It was Debbie.

'I'm sorry that you're not starting.'

That was nice of her.

'It's fine Debbie. Honestly.'

'You should be starting,' she said.

'No I shouldn't,' I said. 'Now go and be brilliant!'

She smiled and ran off to take up her position at right half-forward.

I caught Mum's eye just before I got to the dug-out. She called me over.

'Are you not starting?' she asked.

'No Mum, I'm not. That's why I'm wearing a track-suit top.'

You can be harder on your Mum than you can be on your friends.

'Why not?' she asked.

'I don't know Mum. I mustn't be good enough.'

'Ah that's not true,' Mum said. 'There must be some other reason.'

She was trying at least.

'I'm sure you'll be on soon.'

She gave me a hug and I let her. Passively. I didn't hug her back. I just allowed my arms hang limp. It wasn't very cool, your mum hugging you on the sideline, but I wasn't against a hug from Mum, the way I was feeling. Even in plain sight. Even before the game. Even with people watching.

I smiled at Mum and made my way back to the dug-out.

I had been beginning to come to terms with not starting before Stephen had said that to Tina and Debbie in the huddle. About switching sides. Our thing. I felt betrayed.

I was upset by it all. I was upset by not starting, I was upset by the fact that Tina was going to be playing my role with Debbie. I felt a little jealous, and that was surprising. I figured out that I was jealous of Tina, that she would be feeding off Debbie and vice versa, when it should have been me.

And that was on top of not starting.

I was also upset by Stephen, by the fact that he hadn't spoken to me before he announced the team, or even after he announced the team. He knew that he was going to drop me, so why didn't he tell me? Big chicken. Or even after he dropped me. He should have told me why.

I had lots of emotions. Anger, jealousy, disappointment, frustration. None of them were good.

Our team were all set, but the Ardart girls were still in a huddle. The referee was blowing his whistle, but still they remained in their huddle.

I had a quick glance down to the far goals, the goals into which we were shooting in the first half, and there was no shadow. I didn't expect to see a shadow. I had imagined it in that game against Croughton. Definitely. It was a dull and murky day that day and there were shadows everywhere.

Still no sign of the game starting, so I left the dug-out and strolled up to the dressing room goals on my own. I walked up behind the goals, and just stood behind the net. I thought of Daddy.

I blocked everything else out, every other sound, and immediately I felt better. You know that you're good enough to start. That's what he would have said. That's all that matters, he would have said. You know that you're good enough. The fact that the manager hasn't started you is not relevant. You will get your chance later on, and you will prove that you're good enough. You know that you will.

I felt good. Enthused. I wanted to get on now. I wanted to get my chance. The Ardart girls had taken up their positions and the referee had thrown the ball in before I got back to the dug-out. Ardart won the throw-in and went on the attack. Their midfielder kicked it long, in towards our goals. Their number 15 got out in front of Rebecca, caught the ball cleanly, bounced it once and kicked it over the bar.

Poor start.

It got worse. Sofia's kick out, intended for Edel, was a little high, and Edel's marker knocked it out of her hands easily. She moved forward and passed it over Robyn's head to their number 14, who was in on goal with only Sofia to beat. Fortunately, she kicked it high. Over the bar. It could have been worse, it could have been a goal. Even so, we were two points down and we hadn't got over the half-way line yet.

But it got better. Sofia kicked the ball long, up towards our midfield, and Lily won it. She passed to Shelley, who ran off her well, and Shelley passed to Tina. Debbie moved forward into the centre, ahead of her marker, but Tina ignored her and shot. She was a long way out, and she didn't have the power. The ball dropped short, into the Ardart goalkeeper's hands, and she was able to clear it to their number five.

Stephen was shouting. Patrick was pacing. There were a good few people at the game too, there was a bit of an atmosphere. I had come around. I was rooting for the girls, but I was also dying to get on. There was a part of me that was wanting Aoife or Ciara to play poorly, so that Stephen would put me on instead of one of them.

That's the plight of the substitute. You want the team

to do well, but you want someone to do poorly so that you can get on. I tried to convince myself that it was only a small part of me that wanted Aoife or Ciara to mess up but, actually, it was most of me. I found myself willing Aoife to get the ball and to give it away, and that wasn't good. And she wasn't really messing up, she couldn't really mess up, she wasn't getting the ball. She didn't touch the ball once in the first ten minutes.

Ciara scored a point and Sinéad scored a point, but Ardart scored three more.

We were five-two down about half way through the first half when Shelley got the ball in midfield. She hopped the ball once, soloed it once, then kicked it forward. Debbie got out in front of her marker and took the ball in her chest. She hopped the ball and went to turn but, as she did, her marker, the Ardart number seven, lifted her arm and struck Debbie in the face. Debbie fell to the ground like a sack of potatoes.

'Referee!'

The referee blew his whistle and pointed for a free for us. He checked on Debbie, then quickly beckoned to our dug-out, to Stephen, to come on. Stephen and Patrick both ran out onto the field, Patrick clutching the medical bag, as all our girls gathered around Debbie, who was still on the ground.

All our girls except Tina. She went over to the Ardart number seven and pushed her. The Ardart girl pushed her back. Tina pushed her again, harder this time. It was a good thing that the referee was there to break it up. It could have got ugly.

The ref was talking sternly to the Ardart girl, but I was more concerned about Debbie. It didn't look good. Debbie was never one to stay on the ground. She'd be up quickly, saying she was grand, even if she wasn't. There were two other adults out on the pitch as well, a man and a woman, probably Debbie's parents.

Slowly, Debbie sat up, which was good news. The man, Debbie's dad, had his arms around her and Stephen was crouching down beside the two of them. Eventually, Debbie got up slowly. Her dad kept his arms around her and the pair of them started to walk over towards us. Stephen ran a few paces ahead of them, and called over.

'Anna!' he shouted.

'Get ready. Quickly.'

Chapter 20

SEMI-INVOLVED

I was conflicted: I was sad for Debbie, and I was a little worried for Debbie, but I was delighted that I was getting to go on. I was delighted that I was going to be involved.

I took off my tracksuit top and stuck my gum shield into my mouth. I went over to Debbie, who was making her way gingerly off the pitch with her mum and dad. There was no blood on her face, which was obviously good, and her nose was straight. Her pretty face was still as pretty as ever, even if her hair was all over the place.

'Are you okay, Debbie?' I bumbled.

It's not easy to talk with a gum shield in your mouth.

Debbie looked at me and smiled. Her teeth were all there, all intact, all straight. Her eyes were not there though. She was vacant. As if she had just woken up from a deep sleep.

'I'm fine, Anna,' she said.

I smiled back at her.

'Go and be brilliant!' she said, and she laughed out loud, like a drunk man would laugh at his own joke.

'Anna!'

Stephen was holding out a piece of paper for me to take.

'Referee!' he shouted at the referee.

The ref looked over and Stephen rolled his hands around each other. I ran out to the ref and gave him the piece of paper.

'Right half-forward!' Stephen shouted after me.

Tina was taking the free as I made my way towards my position, right half-forward. She steadied herself and kicked. It looked like it was going wide on the right side, but it was curling. It curled in and just made it inside the right post and just over the crossbar. It landed on top of the net on the far side of the crossbar.

'Great score, Tina!'

Five three. Just two points in it now.

It's never easy when you come on as a sub. You have

to get your bearings, you have to get up to the speed of the game quickly. Everyone else has settled into the match, they have settled into the rhythm of the game. When you come on as a sub, you have to get into your rhythm quickly.

'Come on, Anna,' said Sinéad as I ran past her towards my position. 'Get stuck in.'

The Ardart girl hit me on the shoulder with her shoulder. What? The game hadn't even re-started and she was hitting me. She looked at me in the eye, as if she was going to kill me. It was the number seven. What was she still doing on the pitch? I thought the ref had sent her off.

The ref was blowing his whistle and running over to us. He pointed to the Ardart number seven and spoke with the whistle still in his mouth, which I imagine is even more difficult than with a gum shield in your mouth.

'Cut it out now,' the ref shouted at the Ardart girl, in her face, as he wagged his finger. 'One more and you're off.'

He blew his whistle again and beckoned to the Ardart goalkeeper to take the kick-out. I looked at the goalie and readied myself for the kick-out, in case the ball would come my way.

And there it was. At first I wasn't sure. I got this surge through my body, like an electric current in reverse, that made my head go light for a second and my legs go weak. The shadow. It was back. My shadow. Again. Behind the goalkeeper, behind the goals. Behind the umpire on the right.

I felt a little scared, a little excited and a little freaked out, but mostly I felt comforted. A lot comforted.

A little shiver went down my spine and I squinted. I tried to focus my gaze so that I could be certain that there was a shadow there. There was. No there wasn't. There was nothing there. But there was. For sure. The shadow. My shadow. Or there was something there. Definitely. Wasn't there?

And just like in the Croughton game, it was difficult to be sure. Today was a different day too, the weather was different, it was brighter than it had been for the Croughton game, it was warmer than it had been for the Croughton game. But still, there appeared to be a shadow there. In the form of a man. Tall and slender, just like Daddy. Just there, behind the goals. Stationary. Not well-defined and not moving. Not clapping or jumping or running. Just there, motionless, calm, quiet, composed.

Daddy?

The kick-out was coming our way. I jumped with the Ardart number seven, but I jumped earlier and I jumped higher, and I caught the ball cleanly. I landed on the ground and moved forward. Sinéad was to my left, calling for the ball, but she was marked, and I was free. I didn't know where my marker had gone, perhaps she had fallen to the ground when she had contested the high ball, but I knew that I was free.

I hopped the ball once, soloed the ball once, hopped the ball again. There were players close to me, there were shouts, but the goals were right there and I was close enough, just outside the 21 and a little to the right of the goals. I slowed a little and shaped to my right a little, and shot. Right-footed. I started the ball out a bit to the right of the goals and tried to curl it in. I made a perfect connection with the ball, it started out exactly where I wanted it to start out, a little to the right of the right-hand post. As soon as the ball left my boot, I knew that it was going over the bar. It sailed over the black spot, straight over the middle of the crossbar, and landed on the ground behind the goals. I turned around and clenched my fist. It wasn't a fist pump, it was just a clenched fist, an involuntary fist-clench, and it wasn't for anyone, it was just for me, just because that was how I felt. I think that it was a mixture of pride and relief, and it swelled up in my chest and moved up through my throat and appeared as a smile on my face.

I love this game.

'Brilliant, Anna!'

'Well done, Anna!'

'Great score, Anna!'

I got back to my position, right half-forward, and readied myself for the kick-out. And there was the shadow again. Definitely there. Behind the goals. He was moving a little this time. It looked like his arms were above his head, and it looked like he was smiling.

How can a shadow smile?

The rest of the first half went well. I got plenty of the ball, I gave lots of passes and I scored another point. Tina scored another one and Amanda got one too. At half-time, we were just one point behind, seven six.

'Well done, girls,' said Stephen as he gathered us together. 'Get a drink there. Is everyone okay? No injuries?'

'How's Debbie?' asked Lily.

'Debbie's fine,' said Stephen. 'She's just gone off to the hospital with Patrick and her parents for a check-up, just to make sure that everything is okay. The best thing that we can do now for Debbie, is go and win this match so that she'll be back for the final. Okay?'

'Okay.'

'Okay?!'

'Okay!'

'OKAY???!!!'

'OKAY!!!'

Tina put one arm around Edel and her other arm around Sinéad. Edel put her arm around Shelley and Sinéad put her arm around Rebecca, and we all put our arms around each other. Suddenly I found myself in among them all, my left arm around Ciara, my right arm around Robyn.

'Who are we?' called Tina.

'Ballymarra!' everybody shouted. I didn't shout. I hadn't really been ready to shout.

'Who are we?' called Tina again.

'Ballymarra!' everybody shouted again, a little more loudly. I joined in this time, but my 'Ballymarra' was more spoken softly than shouted loudly.

'Who are we?' Tina shouted out loud.

'Ballymarra! Ballymarra! Ballymarra!'

By the time we got to the third 'Ballymarra', I was shouting at the top of my voice!

As a rallying cry, it worked all right.

I looked for my shadow as I ran out onto the pitch. It looked like there was nothing behind the far goals, the goals into which we had been shooting in the first half. My heart sank. I looked up to the goals that were closest to the dressing room though, and there it was. My insides did a little somersault. There definitely appeared to be something there. It was more than my imagination. Behind the road goals, the Ardart goals, the goals into which we were shooting in the second half.

It gave me a full feeling. I felt confident. I felt sure that I would do the right things, make the right decisions. I pulled the green sock on my left leg up so that I was sure that it was covering the orange sock that was underneath, and the referee threw the ball in.

The second half started well for us. Shelley won the throw-in and passed to Sinéad, who passed to Tina, who kicked it over the bar. We were level before we had played a minute of the second half.

After that, we dominated. I scored another point and Tina scored two, one from a free, and Sinéad got one, during which time Ardart only scored one. Then Aoife got a goal. It was a messy goal, it was a shot for a point by Sinéad that fell short, but the goalkeeper dropped it and Aoife was there to kick it into the net. It doesn't matter, they all count, and it was great for Aoife to score a goal.

About half-way through the second half, Stephen

moved Tina back into midfield, and he moved Shelley to left half-forward. And he took Ciara off and put Sue on.

I played very well. I knew that I did. I didn't tell anyone that I played very well, and when people told me afterwards that I was great, I just shrugged and smiled and said that the whole team was great, but I knew that I had been good. I felt assured in everything that I did. When I contested a ball, I fully expected to win it. When I passed, I expected my pass to hit my target's chest. When I shot, I expected to score. And when I did score, the shadow behind the goals moved or smiled or waved and once I thought that he was dancing.

Tina played well, but she was her usual selfish self. She had the ball on the left once, I made a run through, I was clean through and just inside her, but she shot. In fairness, she scored a point, but she was at a difficult angle, and I was clean through for a goal. The pass was the correct option but, when you are Tina, the pass is rarely the correct option.

Another time she was being crowded by three or four Ardart girls, I was just behind her calling for the ball. I had a clear shot, about fifteen metres out and straight in front of the goals, but she chose to turn back into the crowd of players, probably hoping that the ref would give her a free. Unfortunately, but correctly, he gave a free against her.

I could have shouted at her, but I didn't. I just smiled and turned to run back to my position.

When the referee blew the final whistle, we were well in front. A goal and 14 points to 10 points. Ardart only scored three points in the second half.

I crouched down on my hunkers. It was only after the final whistle had blown that I realised how tired I was. I looked down the pitch, and my shadow was there. Still there, behind the road goals. Still just a blur. I wasn't sure if he was moving or not now, but he was definitely smiling. You could tell. His arms were not up in the air, they were against his chest or down by his side or cupped against his mouth. I felt warm and happy and sad and lonely all at the same time.

A hand touched my shoulder.

'Well done,' said the Ardart number seven, as she stretched her hand out.

I stood up and shook her hand.

'You were very good,' she said. 'You deserved it.'

'Well played yourself,' I said.

'And, em,' she said hesitantly. 'Is your friend all right?'

I looked at her blankly.

'Your friend? Who had to go off? Number 10?'

Debbie? Was she asking about Debbie?

'Debbie?' I asked out loud.

'Yeah, Debbie. I think they were saying Debbie. Do you know if she is okay?'

'I'd say she is,' I said. 'I hope she is. They said at half-time that they were just taking her in for a check-up.'

'Well,' said the Ardart girl. 'Tell her I'm sorry. It was an accident. I didn't mean to hurt her.'

I smiled at her. That was good of her, and it seemed like she really meant it.

'I'll tell her.'

Robyn and Rebecca were racing towards me, jumping and running and shouting at the same time. I wasn't sure whether I should prepare to jump with them, try to jump in unison with them, or run away from them. I wasn't sure which course of action would be safer. In an instant, I decided to take my chances and join in the jumping. Robyn's shoulder hit my chin as we started jumping together and hugging each other, but it wasn't sore and I didn't really care anyway.

Before we knew it, there were eight or nine or ten or eleven girls with us, all in a heap, all jumping and laughing and shouting together. Some were out of sync with the main group, but nobody seemed to care. Everyone was just caught up in the excitement.

I looked over towards the sideline, and there was Mum, clapping and smiling and maybe crying. It was difficult to tell. She stopped clapping when she knew that I was looking over at her and put her two thumbs up. She mouthed something to me, but I couldn't tell what it was, so I mouthed back:

'What?'

I whispered it and mouthed it.

'You were brilliant,' her mouth said. I think. Deliberately and exaggeratedly.

I wanted to put my two thumbs up back at her, but my arms were locked in embraces with the girls as we all jumped and shouted together. I couldn't get my arms back. So I just smiled back at Mum and said 'Yay'.

'Yay!' she said back.

Then we lined up behind Tina and, one by one, shook hands with the Ardart girls.

Chapter 21

• • • • • • •

NOT EASY

I had just hung up on Sally when I heard the front door opening downstairs. Sally was in great form. She told William that she liked him, and William told her that he liked her back. That was massive news!

There was lots of other news from Mountbridge. Sally was settling into secondary school a little bit better now than she had been at the start of the year. Kate and Evelyn were good, but Hannah was being a bit of a pain. Hannah had started to hang out with these other girls, girls who had their noses pierced and who smoked at the bus stop on the way home, and she was ignoring Sally a bit in school. Sally was sad about it, but if that's the way that Hannah wanted to be, she figured, then there was nothing she could do about it.

Sally had started to hang out a bit with Sarah Connolly. I knew Sarah Connolly, she was sweet, but she was more into nails and hair than she was into football. That was fine, it was just that I didn't have that much in common with her. Sally seemed to like her though, and that was fine with me too. Well, it was kind of fine.

I have to admit, I did feel a little bit jealous, which was ridiculous. How could I be jealous of someone for hanging out with Sally? Sally probably detected it in me – Sally knows me so well – and she assured me that Sarah wasn't going to be replacing me. We had a good laugh about that. Sarah Connolly: The New Anna Hogan! We laughed so much that my tummy ached. I don't laugh like that with anyone in Ballymarra.

They were out of the Galway championship too. They were beaten by Galderry in the quarter-final. It was a close game, but they lost by four points in the end. Everybody was disappointed. Sally was gutted.

She was delighted to hear that we had won our semi-final though, and that I had played well. (She asked me how I had played and I couldn't lie!) She was definitely going to come to the final. That would be great, to have Sally there at the final. She said that she'd talk to her mum.

She missed me. I missed her too.

I really missed her.

I heard the front door closing, and I heard voices. Hushed voices. Mum's and someone else's. It was a male voice, but it wasn't Grandad. I strained my ears. It sounded like Stephen.

'I still don't fully understand,' Mum was saying. Almost whispering.

'I know,' the male voice said. Probably Stephen. 'It was stupid.'

'Stupid is right,' Mum said.

'I don't know what I was thinking,' the male voice said.

Definitely Stephen.

The kitchen door opened and the voices fell silent. I didn't hear the kitchen door closing though, so I slowly and quietly opened my bedroom door, and I inched down the stairs to about half-way down, about six or seven steps from the bottom, and I sat down on the step. I could hear the television in the sitting room, just about. Granny or Grandad or both of them were prob-ably in there. Grandad was probably asleep. But I could hear Mum and Stephen from the open-doored kitchen more clearly. I don't know why they didn't close the door. Maybe Mum had stormed into the room and Stephen had just followed, unsure if he was allowed to close the door or not.

Were they breaking up? Were they even together enough to be able to break up?

'I should have started her,' Stephen said.

Maybe they weren't breaking up. Pity.

'But you didn't,' Mum said.

'I know,' Stephen said. 'I was just under so much pressure.'

'From a teenager?' Mum asked.

Silence.

'From your teenage daughter?' Mum asked, more pointedly.

'It wasn't just pressure,' Stephen said. 'She made a good case too. That she and Debbie could play very well together. That they had been playing together for years. That Anna had only just started to play with them, and that she didn't understand properly how Debbie played.'

'And yet,' Mum said. 'Correct me if I'm wrong here, but Anna and Debbie had been playing together in training? And they had been playing well together? Not Tina and Debbie?'

Silence. Stephen probably nodded.

'At a couple of training sessions?'

'Four,' said Stephen quietly.

'And Tina and Debbie had never played together like that? Switching sides? Never once in training?'

Silence again.

'And you thought that it would be a good idea to try something new in a game, a big game, that you had never tried in training, and to abandon something that had been working well in training in order to facilitate that?'

Silence. Probably nodding.

'I'm no football coach,' Mum said, 'but that doesn't make any sense to me.'

Go Mum!

'I know,' Stephen said. 'It doesn't make any sense to me now either, looking back on it. But it made sense to me at the time.'

Mum didn't say anything. I don't know if she was nodding or thinking or glowering. She doesn't need to say anything when she is glowering. I know that glower, and I almost felt sorry for Stephen if he was on the receiving end of one of Mum's glowers now.

'And it wasn't just that I was getting pressure from Tina,' Stephen said. 'I was getting pressure from Jennifer as well. She was saying that Tina wasn't playing well since Anna joined the team. That she wasn't enjoying it. My own daughter. Her daughter. What was I doing managing the team in a way that made my own daughter unhappy.'

'Seriously?' said Mum in that incredulous voice that can makes you feel very small.

'I know,' said Stephen. 'It's ridiculous. I know that it's ridiculous now, looking back on it. I just wasn't thinking straight at the time. She can be so convincing though. So manipulative.'

'So that's why you didn't even start Anna?' Mum asked.

Silence again.

'Is Anna one of the best players on the team?'

Silence yet again. That was frustrating. I definitely wanted to know the answer to that one.

'So, you left one of your best players on the sideline because you were convinced that it was the correct thing to do by your fourteen-year-old daughter and your estranged wife, who knows even less about football than I do, as far as I can make out.'

Silence again. There was the clinking of some cups and the sound of a kettle being filled.

'So why didn't you talk to Anna beforehand?' Mum asked suddenly. 'Isn't that the done thing? If you are dropping a player, you talk to them beforehand? Or even afterwards?'

'It is,' Stephen said, quite loudly, over the sound of the kettle coming to the boil. 'Of course it is. It's the right thing. But I didn't know what to say to Anna. I didn't know how to tell her. Or you. I knew that she would be disappointed. And, I wasn't really sure what my rationale was. When it came to it, I didn't really know why I was dropping her.'

The sound of the kettle got louder, and I really couldn't make out what they were saying for a few seconds. It appeared that they were still talking about the game. Something about me starting in the corner. Or not starting in the corner as it turned out. Mum said something about me only coming on because of poor Debbie's injury. The kettle clicked.

'How is Debbie?' Mum asked.

'She's not bad,' Stephen said. 'She should be back training next week.'

I heard the sound of the water being poured into the teapot.

'I would have brought her on, Emma,' said Stephen. 'You know that I would. Definitely at half-time. Or early in the second half.'

'I don't know that,' said Mum. 'And anyway, it's not about that. Really. I'm not one of those mothers who can't see beyond her daughter. And I don't know the nuances of Gaelic football. Not like Jack did. I don't know the technical stuff.'

She paused. Silence for a few seconds. Then Mum spoke again.

'I don't even know what to say to Anna after a game or a training session. I don't know what questions to ask her. I try to ask the right questions, but I can see that they are not the right questions. I can tell by her reaction. It's like she is waiting for me to ask her the questions that she wants to answer, but I don't. And she gets disappointed and annoyed, and then I get sad and frustrated. Her dad always asked the right questions.'

I could tell that Mum was getting a little bit teary. Poor Mum. She paused again, then continued.

'They'd go into their own little world after a game and talk for ages. It was amazing. They would both remember everything that happened in a game. Absolutely everything. Not just goals or points, or even frees or near-misses, but passes and tackles and moves, and sometimes things that happened before a kick-out, while the ball wasn't even in play. I was never part of that world. Well, I was a part of it, they included me, but I could not contribute to it. Not with them. Not like them. That was their little world. I used to just look at the pair of them and smile and marvel at how alike they were.'

I felt like running down the stairs and into the kitchen and throwing my arms around Mum.

'But I have to be a part of it now. I have no option. And I want to be. I'm learning about it. I want to learn. And I know that Anna is good. Even I can tell that she is one of the better players on the team. And it wasn't fair on her, to leave her on the sideline like that, without even an explanation.'

She cleared her throat. She was moving from sad to annoyed.

'And this is as much about you Stephen as it is about Anna. For you to leave a good player on the sidelines, just to appease Tina and Jennifer. A player who is more concerned about herself than she is about the team, and a mother who doesn't even go to games, and who doesn't know very much about Gaelic football as far as I can see. That doesn't make sense to me. And it doesn't send a good message to Anna. Or, for that matter, to Tina or to Jennifer.'

They were both silent for a second or two. Stephen eventually spoke. Or croaked.

'I know.'

There was more silence. I didn't know if they were

looking at each other or pouring their tea or drinking their tea.

'Look Stephen,' said Mum quietly. 'I'm not sure that this is going to work out.'

Her voice got louder as she spoke, as if she was walking towards the open door. Crap! I stood up quickly and blinked. As quickly and as quietly as I could, I scampered up the stairs. It's hard to be quick and quiet while running up the stairs. Luckily, bare feet on carpet don't make that much noise, and I knew enough to jump over the creaky stair, the third one from the top.

Quietly but firmly, the kitchen door closed.

Chapter 22

TROUBLE AT TRAINING

Big week, the week before the final. Stephen decided that we would train three times that week, Monday, Wednesday and Friday. There was a good atmosphere around the place. Everyone was in good form, everyone was excited. Stephen tried to downplay everything. It was just another game. When the whistle went, it was the same as the previous game, and the one before that, and the one before that. And we had won all those. He didn't speak about what was at stake, about the fact that Ballymarra had never won an under-age girls' championship. Under any age. We all knew though.

Monday's session was tough enough, plenty of running, but Wednesday's session was nice, mainly ball work. We did lots of passing and shooting though, the whole team, even the defenders. Although we did decide that, if Robyn was to get within shooting range, she should pass. There was a reason why she was full-back and not full-forward.

Robyn laughed.

I got to training early on Friday evening. I told Mum that I wanted to get there early. It was a big training session, the last one before the final.

Also, I usually got to training and to matches just on time. Training at 7.00pm, I'd arrive at 7.00pm, but nearly everybody would be there already. Game at 2.00pm, be there by 1.30pm, I'd be there at 1.30pm, but nearly everybody would be there when I walked into the dressing room. It meant that I was always the new person when I arrived.

I know why I did it. I did it because I wanted to minimise the amount of time that I would spend there, before the training started or before preparations for the game began. I figured that I would have nobody to talk to, so the less time that I could spend there, on my own, talking to nobody, the better.

I was starting to think though that it might be better

221

to arrive earlier. That it might be easier if I arrived earlier.

Mum dropped me to the pitch at 6.30pm. She just dropped me to the gate. We could see Stephen on the pitch, putting out flags and cones. I thought that Mum might come in to see him, but she didn't. I said it to her.

'Are you not coming in to see Stephen?'

'No, pet, I'm not.'

'Okay. Bye.'

'Bye, pet.'

I didn't give her a kiss. I give Mum a kiss sometimes when I am getting out of the car, but going to training, on a Friday evening, with people around, and when she's going to be picking me up again an hour and a half or two hours later, I generally don't.

'Train well,' Mum said as I got out of the car. 'Have fun.'

She never said have fun. It was as if she didn't want me to go.

'See you later,' she said. 'Half eight isn't it?'

'Yes, Mum,' I said as I closed the door. 'It always is.'

Stephen was getting the bibs out of the bag when I walked onto the pitch.

I hadn't really spoken to Stephen since that evening in our house, since Mum had given out to him for leaving me out of the starting team. And I hadn't really spoken to him that evening either. I hadn't even really seen him. I had just heard him.

I had seen him at training and all, but I hadn't really spoken to him, and he hadn't really spoken to me. Not to say anything more than 'Go, Anna' anyway, when it was my turn to sprint. Or 'Anna, you mark Sandra'. Or 'Anna, on the left'.

I don't think Mum had seen much of Stephen either. I wasn't aware that she had seen him at all actually. So when she had said to Stephen that she wasn't sure if this – whatever this was – was going to work out, she obviously hadn't been joking.

'Hi, Stephen,' I called.

He looked up and saw me. First he looked startled, a little scared even. Then he smiled and looked at his wrist.

'Hi, Anna,' he said with a laugh. 'What time do you call this?'

'Ha, ha,' I said. 'It's half six.'

'You know training is at seven, right?' Stephen joked.

'I know,' I said. 'I just figured that I'd get here early.'

'Okay good,' he said. 'There are balls over at the dug-out there with the girls if you want to have a kick around.'

Sofia and Aoife were over at the dugout. They weren't

kicking a ball around though, they were just standing there, chatting. This was nice. Being early. It was a lot less intimidating arriving when there were only two girls there than it was arriving when there were fifteen girls there.

As I approached the dugout, I started to get nervous. What if Sofia and Aoife didn't talk to me? What if they didn't include me in their conversation? They were good friends, they would probably be talking about something that didn't concern me. And I had a feeling that Aoife didn't really like me. Why would she like me? I had probably pushed her out of her guaranteed place on the starting fifteen. I was the reason why she didn't start in some games.

Also, I would have nothing to contribute to their conversation. So I would be just standing there, one of three, as the other two would be chatting. Standing there, talking to nobody with just three of us there. Nowhere to hide. That would be way worse than standing there talking to nobody with twenty of us there.

And then someone else would arrive, and they would join in the conversation with Sofia and Aoife, and I would still be left there, talking to nobody. This was awful. I could feel myself sweating. This was a terrible idea, coming to training early. I wanted to reverse time and be at home and plan to arrive at seven.

'Hi girls,' I said.

There was a moment, a fraction of a second, when the two girls looked at me and neither of them spoke. It was just a moment, probably a half a second, less than half a second, but it was a worrying moment. They could have completely ignored me and gone back to their conversation. Then Sofia spoke.

'Hi, Anna,' she said warmly.

'Hi, Anna,' Aoife said, also fairly warmly.

Relief.

'We're just talking about Fire,' said Sofia.

'Are you going?' she asked me.

I looked at her blankly.

'The Christmas disco?'

'Oh yeah,' I said hesitantly.

'Fire? Yeah.'

I had heard of it. The Christmas disco in the Market Hotel. To be honest, I hadn't even considered going to it, or asking Mum if I could go to it.

'I don't know,' I said honestly.

'You should go!' said Aoife. 'We should all go. The whole team. It would be great fun if we all went. My mum said that if Sofia's mum lets her go, then I can go.'

This was refreshing, Aoife talking about her mum

letting her or not letting her go to something. It was honest. None of this, I'll go if I want to go. None of this, I don't have to get permission from my mum. That stuff is for kids and I'm not a kid. I decided there and then that I liked Aoife. I went from having no real opinion on her, being a little afraid to talk to her, being a little embarrassed that I was taking her place on the team, at least some of the time, to liking her in an instant.

Sofia looked a little bit embarrassed admittedly.

'I'd say I'll be allowed to go all right,' she said sheepishly.

'Here's Debbie,' said Aoife suddenly.

I looked around over my left shoulder and, sure enough, Debbie was walking towards us. We watched her for a few seconds. She was too far away for us to say anything to her without shouting. She saw us watching her and I think she smiled. It was difficult to tell.

'Hi, Debbie,' Sofia called first. 'How are you?'

Debbie took a few more steps before she tried to respond. Just to take her closer to us probably, so that she wouldn't have to shout too loudly.

'I'm good thanks,' she said, quite loudly.

She was just about audible.

'That's great,' said Sofia.

I didn't say anything. I was just smiling. I was surprised at how happy I was to see Debbie.

'Hi, Debbie,' said Aoife.

'Hi, Aoife,' said Debbie.

I didn't know what to say. Debbie looked at me, probably saw me grinning like a Cheshire cat, and smiled.

'It's great to see you, Debbie,' I said eventually.

I wanted to hug her, but that would have been completely uncool and absolutely inappropriate.

'Great to see you too, Anna.'

She's so nice.

'How are you feeling?' asked Sofia.

'I'm good thanks,' said Debbie. 'I'm doing well.'

'You were concussed, right?'

'I was,' said Debbie, quietly and a little embarrassedly, even though she had nothing to be embarrassed about.

'What does that mean exactly?' asked Aoife. 'Concussed? Like, what did it feel like?'

'It's just a mild brain injury,' said Debbie. 'It sounds worse than it is. Really. I was just a bit dazed. I felt like I was dreaming. When I got the knock on the head, I could see my dreams from the night before. Or even the week before. Then the whole game seemed like it was a dream.'

'Wow,' said Aoife. 'That's pretty cool!'

'Yeah it was Aoife,' said Debbie softly.

'And were you in hospital for long?'

'No, just overnight,' said Debbie. 'The weird thing was though, I would come to my senses, and I would think, wow that was weird, all of that seems like it was a dream. But I'm okay now. I know what I'm doing. I'm in the real world. I'm not dreaming now. And then a few minutes later, it would also seem like *that* was a dream. And then I would think, wow, that was even weirder. And then that would seem like it was a dream too.'

'That's crazy!' I exclaimed, almost involuntarily.

'It was a bit crazy all right,' said Debbie. 'I tried to explain that to the nurses, and they seemed to under-stand. It's normal for someone with concussion. Mild concussion. That's why they kept me in overnight.'

'And were they happy for you to go back playing football?' I asked.

'Yeah. They said that I shouldn't play for ten days or two weeks, but they were happy that that was long enough.'

I counted the days since the game. Twelve. This was the twelfth day.

'This is the twelfth day,' I said out loud.

'I know,' said Debbie with a smile. 'That's more than ten days, right?'

We all laughed. Fair play to Debbie. She's so nice. So likeable. So popular. It was great that she was back. Lily and Rebecca and Amanda and Shelley had all arrived as Debbie was speaking, and they were all standing around, listening to Debbie's story. Rebecca touched my back as Debbie was speaking and smiled. Hi.

Suddenly, Debbie realised that everybody was listening to her.

'Right,' she said as she clapped her hands together. 'That's enough of that! Anyone want to have a kick around?'

She was right. We were there to train. I turned around and walked towards the dug-out, where the balls were. As I picked up one of the balls, Rebecca appeared beside me.

'Wanna pair up?' she asked.

'Hi, Rebecca,' I said. 'Of course.'

Robyn obviously hadn't arrived yet. I didn't mind. I didn't mind being Rebecca's second choice. I liked Rebecca. She was straight up. What you saw was what you got with her. There were no sides to her, no angles. Her kick passes weren't that accurate, but you could allow her that.

I got a ball and took my place on the 21. Rebecca went to the end line, and I passed to her. Right foot.

Bang, landed on her chest. She kicked it back to me, up in the air but straight towards me. The ball bounced about three metres from me, and I caught it before it bounced again.

'So are you going to Fire?' Rebecca shouted.

'I don't know,' I said, as I landed the ball in Rebecca's chest again.

'Are you?'

'I think so,' she said. 'I hope so. It should be great fun.'

Her pass went astray, a little over to my right, so that I had to run after it.

'Sorry,' she shouted.

The place was filling up now. Ciara and Sinéad and Sandra and Edel had arrived. As they arrived, the girls were taking their places either on the end line or on the 21, opposite a partner, and passing. It was a good idea to get there early. And Robyn. Robyn came over towards us, looking a little uncertain.

'Here, Robyn,' I said. 'Join in with us. We'll make it a triangle.'

Both Rebecca and Robyn appeared to be happy about that. I noticed Tina arriving behind me. Maybe it was my imagination, but there always appeared to be a different atmosphere when Tina was present. There was a coldness about the atmosphere when she was there.

A sense of trepidation. Unease. Fear even. Or maybe it was just me who was a little bit afraid.

Sinéad had been passing to Amanda down at the bottom of the line, Sinéad on the 21, Amanda on the end line, but she left her and went over to Tina as soon as Tina arrived. Amanda was left standing there on the end line, holding a ball, with no partner. I caught Robyn's pass and kicked to Rebecca, and still Amanda was standing there. No sign of Patrick, no sign of Stephen. He was up at the half-way line, still setting up some cones and flags. Looked like a complicated drill.

I caught another pass from Robyn and kicked to Rebecca. Still Amanda was on her own. Sinéad and Tina were over at the dug-out, just talking.

'Here, I'm going to pair up with Amanda,' I said to Robyn and Rebecca. 'She has no partner.'

'Okay,' said Robyn.

'Hey Amanda,' I called to her, as I took my place on the 21 opposite her. 'Wanna pair up?'

'Sure.'

She seemed happy about that. It was the right thing to do. Sinéad was going to pair with Tina anyway, even after they had finished their little chat.

'I heard you talking about Fire,' said Amanda.

'Yeah,' I said a little reluctantly. Fire wasn't on my

radar until fifteen minutes earlier. I didn't even really know what it was. Now it seemed that it was all anybody wanted to talk about.

'I'm not sure if I'm going to be able to go.'

'I was there last time,' said Amanda. 'At the end of the year. It's great. We should all go.'

'Hey, Anna.'

It was Tina. She had crept up behind me. I hadn't even noticed. She was walking towards me now, about ten metres away from me. Sinéad was a couple of steps behind her. Tina looked to her side and motioned with her head for Sinéad to catch up.

I caught Amanda's pass and kicked the ball back to her.

'Hi, Tina,' I said, trying to conceal the nervousness in my voice.

'Your mother's a slut.'

What? What had Tina just said? Had she just called my mother a slut?

'What?'

I turned immediately to face Tina. I could hear the ball bounce beside me, but I wasn't concerned about passing to Amanda now.

Tina was standing there, most of her body weight on her right leg, that stupid pose that she does, with that stupid grin on her face. She didn't say anything. She just looked back at me. Brazen. Staring me down. She probably practises that look and that stance and that pose and that stupid grin in the mirror for hours.

'What did you just say?' I asked again, more quietly and more calmly than I thought possible.

By now, Sinéad was standing beside Tina. She was looking a little sheepish. The pair of them were close to me now, not quite within touching distance, but not far from touching distance. About one long step away.

'I said, your mother's a slut.'

She said it again. I hadn't misheard. What a cow. Why was she saying that? Why was she calling my mother names? Was it because my mum was seeing her dad? Or because my mum had broken up with her dad? Had they broken up or not? I didn't know.

Thoughts raced through my head in fractions of seconds, thoughts and emotions, tumbling over each other, screaming for attention. I was a bit baffled and a bit scared but, most of all, I was enraged. She could insult me all she wanted, challenge me to fights, post stuff about me on-line. But bringing Mum into it stirred something inside me. I felt this huge sense of responsibility, a need to defend Mum. I had to defend Mum.

The rage inside me gathered momentum. Mum, and

all she had been through, and all she had done for me, and all she had to cope with. And this stupid little cow calling her names. She and her timid dad, her feeble dad. Mum was ten times the person that Stephen was. And here's his daughter, calling her a slut.

The rage engulfed me. I just saw red. It wasn't helped by Tina's stupid stance, her stupid smirk, her stupid pose. I took a step towards her, left foot forward and, before I really knew what I was doing, I was swinging my right hand. I could see the shock in Tina's face as I swung. The stupid grin was gone, the smugness in her eyes had disappeared. All I saw was fright, astonishment, panic.

It was a strange feeling, fist on face. I had never punched anyone in the face before, so it was new to me. I was surprised at how it felt, knuckle on skin. I could feel the pudginess of Tina's cheek first, and then I could feel my clenched fist connecting with something hard. And I have to admit, it felt good. It felt satisfying. More satisfying than it really should have.

Tina was knocked sideways. She rocked to her right, and I thought that she was going to remain upright, but she didn't. Her head moved to her right, followed by her neck, and then her left shoulder and, in an instant, she was gone beyond the point of equilibrium. Her centre of gravity moved to the right and, from that point, she was always going to fall to the ground. Her left leg came up off the ground as her right leg buckled.

It all happened so slowly, but so quickly at the same time. One minute, I was standing there, passing the ball to Amanda, talking about Fire, wondering if Mum would let me go and, even if she would, wondering if I actually wanted to go. The next, I was standing there looking down at Tina who was stretched out on the ground, wondering if she was alive or dead or conscious or semi-conscious, and not really caring whether she was or wasn't.

The knuckles on my right hand felt a little sore.

Chapter 23

SERIOUSLY ANNA

I could hear the voices in the hall downstairs, but I couldn't really tell what they were saying. I didn't try to hear.

Training had been abandoned. I felt partially responsible for that. Or wholly responsible. If I hadn't punched stupid Tina in the face, training would have gone ahead as usual. Then again, if Tina hadn't called Mum a slut, I wouldn't have punched her in her stupid face.

Chaos followed. Shouting and screaming and crying. Bedlam. Before I knew what was happening, there was a crowd of people around me and Tina. Most of the girls gathered around Tina, but some of them came to me.

'Are you okay, Anna?'

Stephen came running over from the other side of the pitch, and Patrick appeared out of nowhere.

'Get her out of here,' Stephen said to Patrick.

Patrick put his hand on my shoulder and I walked with him towards the gate, towards his car. I didn't turn around to look at Tina. I didn't ask how she was before I left. I didn't really care. I didn't apologise.

She was sitting up by the time I turned to leave with Patrick, so at least I knew that she wasn't unconscious. Or dead. That wouldn't have been good. Imagine I had killed Tina.

Patrick hardly said a word to me on the way home in the car. I just got into his car, into the passenger seat, and put on my seat belt. He got into the driver's seat and just started to drive.

'Castle Road,' Patrick said. 'Right?'

I nodded.

I was comfortable with the silence. I suspected that Patrick was annoyed with me, but I didn't feel that he was annoyed with me. I had stepped out of line. I knew that. You can't go around boxing people in the face, no matter what they say. I had boxed his star player. And I had ruined his training session, his last training session before the final.

Patrick just drove. I didn't look over at him, I didn't know what his facial expression was, but there wasn't a bad atmosphere in the car. It wasn't tense.

'What number?' he asked as we turned onto Castle Road.

'Twenty-five,' I said.

We stopped outside our house and I opened the passenger door.

'Anna,' Patrick said suddenly.

I stopped, door half-open, and looked at him.

'What happened there? What you did.'

I braced myself.

'It might not have been a bad thing.'

I smiled and got out of the car. Patrick got out of the driver's side, and we walked up our short driveway.

'Now, if you ever tell anybody that I said that, I'll deny it. You know that, don't you?'

I nodded. Patrick was cool.

Granny opened the door.

'Hi, pet. Hi, Patrick. Is everything okay?'

'Everything is good thanks, Mrs Murtagh,' said Patrick.

'Is Emma here?'

'She is,' said Granny. 'Of course. Emma!'

I sat on the bottom stair and had just finished taking off my boots when Mum came into the hall from the kitchen.

'Hi, pet,' she said, before she saw Patrick.

'Hi, Patrick,' she said when she saw him. 'Is everything all right?'

'Everything is fine,' said Patrick.

I ran up the stairs in my socks.

'Just a small incident at training,' I heard him say before I closed my bedroom door.

☣ ☣ ☣

I had my pyjamas on by the time I heard the front door opening again and Mum saying goodbye to Patrick. I wasn't doing anything. I wasn't reading and I wasn't listening to music, and I had turned my phone off. I had no interest in reading the messages that I was sure to receive.

I was just there, on my bed, my head propped up against the headboard, half-lying, half-sitting, staring at the pile of clean laundry that Mum had obviously put at the bottom of my bed earlier: my jeans, my navy hoodie, my green top and my black football shorts, with my green football socks and two pairs of my white sports socks perched on top.

The front door closed and I heard Mum's footsteps, coming up the stairs. Soft steps, but firm steps. One at a time. I was a little bit nervous. I could be in trouble here. Then the slight squeak of the handle on my door being pushed down. She didn't knock. She knocks sometimes, but not always. The door opened and Mum's face appeared, not a smiling face, but not an overly angry face either. I was a little bit relieved.

'Seriously Anna,' she said.

I didn't say anything. I just fixed my gaze on the pile of laundry that was at the bottom of my bed.

'You can't go around punching people,' Mum said.

'But it was Tina,' I said.

'It doesn't matter who it was. You can't just punch people in the face.'

'But she …'

'I don't care what she did,' said Mum.

'It isn't what she did!' I protested. 'It's what she said!'

'I don't care what she said. You can't just punch people. You can't box people. You shouldn't hit anybody. Ever. No matter what.'

'You weren't there,' I said. 'You don't know what happened.'

'I know I wasn't there. But I do know that you can't

go around hitting people. That doesn't solve anything. And now look what's happened? No training session. Your last training session before the final. And you will probably be dropped from the team.'

I hadn't thought of that.

'Did Patrick say that?'

'No he didn't. But think about it. How can Stephen put you on the team now after this? How can he put you and Tina on the same team? And you're the one who caused this.'

'I didn't.'

'You didn't?'

'No. Tina did. If she hadn't said what she said, I wouldn't have punched her.'

'So it's Tina's fault? It's Tina's fault that you punched her and nearly broke her jaw?'

'Yes!'

'Really?! Really Anna?! The person you punched in the face, it's her fault that you punched her in the face?!'

'I can't believe you're taking Tina's side!'

'I'm not taking Tina's side,' Mum said, some emotion creeping into her voice. 'I'm just pointing out the reality. You punched her. You're the aggressor. You threw the punch. I can't believe you can't see that.'

'And I can't believe that you're taking Tina's side over

mine! Your own daughter!'

'I'm not taking sides,' said Mum, her voice raised a little now. 'You hit another person. You're in the wrong.'

'How can you say that I'm in the wrong when you won't even listen to me,' I shouted.

'Don't raise your voice at me.'

'You don't even want to hear my side of the story!' I was getting myself upset now. 'You don't even want to hear what actually happened? Why I punched her in her stupid face?'

'You can't go around punching people!'

Mum was shouting now.

'You want to know why I punched her?'

'No I don't! It doesn't matter!'

'You don't want to know why? You don't even want to hear it from my point of view?'

'No I don't!'

This was infuriating. So frustrating.

'And you're taking somebody else's side against me?'

'So you say.'

Now I was going to explode.

'Daddy would never take somebody else's side!'

As soon as the words were out, I regretted saying them. Or shouting them. I turned over sharply on my bed, onto my stomach, and buried by face in my pillow.

I was sobbing now. Partly because I was frustrated that Mum wouldn't listen to me. Partly because of what had happened. I had been upset by it all, I had just managed to hold it all together. Until now. Partly because I knew that I had upset Mum. Partly because I missed Daddy.

Most things were at least partly because I missed Daddy.

I just lay there sobbing, my head in my pillow. I didn't know what Mum was going to do. She didn't shout back at me anyway, which was good. She could have just got up and left the room, but that wouldn't be her style. Maybe she was crying herself. Maybe she was thinking about what she was going to do.

I wanted her to grab me and hug me, but I didn't really think that she would. We had never had a shouting match like that before, so I didn't know how she was going to react.

Eventually, after what seemed like an age, she put her hand gently on my shoulder. I turned around. She was looking at me softly, with her beautiful blue eyes, slightly red now.

I sat up and threw my arms around her. She hugged me back tightly. She put her hand on the back of my head and kissed my wet cheek, just beside my right ear.

We just stayed there like that for a few minutes,

both of us sniffling, neither of us loosening our grips. I wanted to speak, but I couldn't. Not immediately anyway. Eventually I figured that I could speak without crying.

'I miss him.'

Mum didn't respond immediately. It took her a few seconds.

'I know you do pet. I miss him too. Desperately.'

We stayed like that for another few minutes until I was sure that I had my emotions under control. I figured that I needed to lighten the mood a little.

'She called you a slut,' I said.

'I know,' said Mum.

Chapter 24

• • • • • •

IMAGINATION RUNNING WILD

'**W**ait,' I said. 'You know? You knew?!'

'Patrick told me.'

'I didn't think Patrick knew.'

'Patrick knows more than everybody thinks he knows.'

We laughed.

'And you still think it was my fault?'

'No, I don't,' said Mum.

I was confused.

'Look, pet,' said Mum. 'When Patrick told me what had happened, that Tina had called me names and that you had punched her in the face, I wanted to run up the stairs and give you a big hug and say, thanks pet. You're brilliant. You're the best daughter in the world. But that would not have been right.'

'Why not?'

'I'm your mother! Firstly, you shouldn't have to defend me. I should be the one who is defending you. And secondly, I have to teach you right from wrong. I can't be teaching you that it's a good thing to punch somebody in the face. Fundamentally, it's wrong. You can't do it.'

'Never?'

'Never.'

'What about, in exceptional circumstances?'

Mum thought for a second.

'The circumstances would have to be very exceptional.'

Mum was smiling.

'Would one of those circumstances be, if somebody called your mother a slut?'

Mum picked up the green football socks that were on top of the pile of clothes and fired them at me. I ducked a little and put my hands up to my ears, and the socks hit the back of my left hand. It was a powerful enough throw. Mum is deceptively strong. Lucky I had my hand over my ear.

She picked up one pair of my little white socks and fired them at me, but she missed. Then she picked up the other pair of white socks and threw, and missed again.

Lucky she wasn't a good shot. I told her that. She laughed. I laughed.

I leaned down to pick up the white socks that were on the floor, and I put them beside my green socks that were on the bed beside me.

'Where are my orange socks, Mum?'

Mum looked at me, a little perplexed.

'They must be still in the wash,' she said.

'Okay,' I said. 'I need them for Sunday though. Is that okay?'

'Okay,' Mum said quietly.

'They're good socks aren't they?' she said slowly.

I nodded. She didn't need an answer. She wasn't looking for an answer.

If she had said something else then, if she had changed the subject, I would have moved on too. Or if she had got up and gone downstairs to make the hot chocolate, I wouldn't have said anything. But she didn't. She just sat there in silence for a few seconds.

I didn't speak because I was thinking of the significance of the socks, and thinking about everything about them, about how well I played when I wore them, about the feeling of confidence that I felt they gave me, and wondering if I should say anything to Mum or not. And about the shadow that seemed to appear when I wore them. The silence went on, so, as much to break the silence as to tell her, I started talking.

'They're special socks,' I said.

Mum nodded.

'No, Mum, really. They're special. I play well when I wear them. I feel confident. I always seem to make the right decisions when I wear them. The ball seems to bounce for me.'

'That's nice, pet.'

She wasn't getting it. I felt the need to impress upon her how special I thought they were.

'I rarely miss. If I shoot when I wear them, I nearly always score. I rarely drop a ball, I hardly ever misplace a pass. I always seem to run into the right space.'

'That's great, pet.'

Mum was sad. She was pensive. She was lost in her own thoughts, probably of Daddy. Not really thinking about what I was saying.

'And when I don't wear them, I play badly.'

She looked at me. It seemed that she was tuning in again.

'Really? That can't be right, pet. You never play badly.'

'But I do,' I said. 'I did. Against Tullafin. I was awful. Remember? I couldn't catch a ball or kick a ball and Stephen took me off.'

'That was just an off day.'

'I know,' I said. 'That's what it was. But I wasn't wearing Daddy's socks. It was a championship game, so I had to wear the green socks.'

'What about against Croughton? You were great against Croughton.'

'I know. Well, I was okay. But that was a challenge match, we didn't have to wear the club socks, so I wore Daddy's!'

'But what about the semi-final?' asked Mum, getting interested now. 'Against Ardart? You came on as a sub and you were great. Did you not wear the green socks that day?'

I was impressed with Mum's knowledge and powers of recollection.

'I did, but I wore Daddy's socks underneath them!'

I said it emphatically, as if I was solving a puzzle. As if this was the final piece of evidence that proved the theorem.

'Really?'

'Really!'

I was nodding enthusiastically.

'That's nice, pet,' said Mum. 'It's nice that you have such confidence when you wear the socks. I'm sure you don't need the socks though. I'm sure that you have that confidence anyway.'

'That's the thing though Mum,' I said. 'I don't. I'm always nervous when I go out onto the pitch. I'm always anxious that things won't go well for me in the game. The first ball, the first catch, the first shot. When Daddy was here, and when I knew that he was there, at the game, behind the goal, I would feel nervous, but I would feel confident. I would be looking forward to the first ball, I would be looking forward to getting going, to getting into the game.'

Mum was just listening. Or it appeared as if Mum was just listening.

'When I knew that Daddy wouldn't be at the games though, I always dreaded the first ball. It was an anxious nervousness that I felt. I wasn't confident. And I wasn't playing well. Now though, when I wear his socks, I feel that confidence again. Nervous, yes, of course, for sure. But looking forward to it. When I don't wear the socks now, I feel anxious and nervous and I play poorly.'

Mum was looking at me, deep in thought. I really wanted to know what she was thinking. She needed prompting though.

'What do you think of that?'

Mum was silent for another second or two.

'I'll tell you what I think,' she said eventually. 'I think that it's in your head. It's like, you are used to Dad being at your games, and now that he can't be at them …'

She stopped for a second. This was upsetting her.

'Mum.'

She put her hand up to stop me.

'Now that he can't be at them,' she continued shakily, 'you needed to find some kind of a replacement. You have found it in those socks.'

A tear escaped from her left eye and made its way surprising quickly down her cheek.

'But it's all in your head, pet,' she said.

She smiled a teary smile.

'You just need some kind of a crutch. Something to give you the confidence to be as good as you can be. But you're a great player. You know that you are. You would be a great player if you were wearing the green socks without Daddy's socks underneath them. Or white socks. Or pink socks with bright blue spots.'

She wasn't really getting it.

'But I have this confidence when I wear the socks. It's as if Daddy is there with me. At the match.'

'But he isn't, pet.'

Another tear.

'It's just in your mind. It's your imagination running wild. You just need to believe in yourself. Know that you are good. You don't need to wear a certain pair of socks. You're good because you're good, because you have the talent and because you train hard. Not because you wear a pair of socks.'

I thought about telling her about the shadow, but decided not to.

'But Mum,' I said. 'I feel like they're a link to Daddy.'

'They're not,' Mum said quite sharply and quite tearfully. 'They're just socks.'

'They're not just socks,' I protested.

'They're just socks,' said Mum.

'They're the socks that Daddy gave me on the day that he died,' I said.

Now it was my turn to get teary.

'They're still just socks,' Mum said, her voice getting louder and shakier at the same time.

'They're not!' I said, more loudly than I had intended. 'When I wear them, I see Daddy's shadow!'

I had said it before I really knew that I was going to say it.

'What?'

I didn't reply. I stayed silent. It probably wasn't a good idea to tell Mum about the shadow. Not when she was so against the idea that the socks gave me confidence.

'You see Daddy's shadow?'

I had to go with this now. Maybe she would understand or, if not understand, then believe me. And, if not believe me, then at least humour me.

'When I wear the socks,' I said slowly, 'not only do I play well, but I see this shadow. It's always behind the goals that we are attacking. Where Daddy used to always stand.'

I paused for a second to look at Mum, try to gauge her reaction, but she was silent. Maybe stunned, maybe intrigued. I continued.

'It's just a haze, and I wasn't sure if it was really something or not, but now I'm sure that it is. It was there for the Croughton game and it was there for the Ardart game when I was on. The only two games in which I wore the orange socks.'

Mum was still silent, her mouth a little open, her eyes deep. I was into this now. I couldn't back out. I couldn't untell her.

'You can just about make it out. It's about the same size as Daddy and the same shape. Tall and lean. And it seems to celebrate when I score or do something good.'

Another tear came down Mum's left cheek. Two tears from her left eye and one from her right eye.

'Stop,' she said suddenly.

'What? Are you okay, Mum?'

'Stop this,' she said. 'Is this a joke? Is this meant to cheer me up? To make me laugh? Because it's not making me laugh.'

Another tear was rolling down her right cheek now.

'Mum, no. This is real. It really happened. I really saw the shadow.'

'You *thought* you saw a shadow,' Mum said abruptly.

She looked stern and serious, even though there were tears in her eyes.

'I'm *sure* I saw a shadow,' I said. 'Twice.'

'This is crazy, Anna.'

She only called me Anna when she was being serious.

'It was your imagination. You saw what you wanted to see. You wanted Dad to be there, so you invented this shadow.'

She spoke through her tears.

'I didn't invent it, Mum. Honestly. It was there. At both games.'

'This is ridiculous,' said Mum, as she wiped her right cheek with the fingers of her right hand.

'I didn't want to believe it either, Mum. I couldn't

believe it. But I do now. It was there. It was as if Daddy was with me.'

'Well, he couldn't have been,' said Mum, quite sharply, quite coldly.

It was strange, that she was able to be so sharp and cold even though she was still crying.

'Daddy is dead. We have to accept that Anna.'

The tears were rolling down her cheeks now.

'He's not coming back.'

She stood up and left the room, and I burst into tears.

Chapter 25

• • • • • •

MEETING

It was quite late when I got down to the kitchen the following morning. I woke up early enough, at about half past eight, and I could hear Granny and Mum and Charlie in the kitchen. Usually when I hear people in the kitchen on a Saturday morning, I bounce out of bed and go down. I like it when we all congregate in the kitchen on a Saturday morning. Also, I think I'm a little bit afraid of missing out on something if I'm not there.

This Saturday morning was different though. My mind was scrambled and I could feel that my eyes were puffy. I had cried myself to sleep. I thought that Mum would come back into me before I went to sleep, but she didn't.

Then there was the whole training incident thing, the fact that I had punched Tina in the face. I wondered what the repercussions of that would be for me. Would I be dropped from the team? Would I be banished from the club? Was Tina going to kill me?

I thought about turning my phone on, but I decided to leave it until after breakfast. Best to eat something first before I faced my phone.

Mum was saying something to Granny as I walked in through the open kitchen door. Something about getting some steak later for dinner.

'Morning,' I muttered sleepily as I walked into the room.

The kitchen floor was cold on my bare feet, so I slid onto the bench at the kitchen table and I tucked my feet up beside me.

'Hi, pet,' said Granny.

'Your hair is messy,' said Charlie.

Mum didn't say anything. She walked over to the kitchen table and sat down beside me on the bench, using her body to push me in further onto the bench and engineering a space so that she could sit beside me. She smiled as she did that.

'You ok?' she asked.

Her eyes were puffy too. I nodded.

'I'm just tired.'

'I came into you last night afterwards,' Mum said.

I looked at her sharply. Did she?

I tried to act cool, but I was delighted to hear her say that. I was delighted that she had come back in. I wanted to hug her, but I didn't. That wouldn't have been cool at all.

'You were fast asleep,' Mum said. 'You looked so peaceful. So angelic.'

I half-smiled and picked up the Corn Flakes box and one of the grey bowls that was on the table in front of me.

'Of course, we know the truth.'

She nudged me with her shoulder. I smiled. Humour her.

'Don't we, Granny?'

'What's that love?'

'Don't we know the truth about Anna? About her angelic nature – or lack thereof?'

'Oh she's angelic all right,' said Granny.

Good old Granny.

'She's our little angel.'

'That's soooo much sugar!' Charlie exclaimed.

'Mummy, look how much sugar Anna is putting on her Corn Flakes!'

I stopped sprinkling the sugar.

The Corn Flakes tasted good. The milk was nice and cold, not too cold, just nice and cold and, Charlie was right, I had put soooo much sugar on. It was nice though, it was sweet, and I was hungry.

Mum got up from the table and walked over towards the cooker.

'Stephen is coming here this morning,' she said.

She said it nonchalantly, as if she was saying that she had put on some toast for me.

'What?!'

I stopped, Corn Flake-full spoon half way between my bowl and my mouth, suspended in mid-air.

'Oh yeah,' said Mum calmly. 'Stephen and Tina. They're coming here this morning.'

'Really?'

I felt weak.

'Why?'

This was not good. A visit from Stephen. An un-scheduled visit from Stephen. I was going to be in trouble. I had punched Tina in the face at training the previous evening. Of course I was going to be in trouble. It seemed like a lot longer ago than just the previous evening. It felt like lots had happened in the meantime.

Maybe Stephen was going to expel me from the club. Or tell me that I wasn't going to play in the final.

'Look, pet,' said Mum softly. 'Stephen wants to clear the air. He wants things to be okay between you and Tina. It's better to do that in private, not in front of everyone. It made sense to me.'

'I hate her,' I said out loud.

'Anna!'

'What?'

'You don't hate her. You don't hate anyone.'

'Yeah,' I said. 'Anyone except Tina stupid Kane.'

'You don't hate her,' said Mum again. 'She has her issues you know. Her mum and dad are broken up. That's not easy for her. She's probably sad. And she's probably spoiled by her mum. She's probably a good kid behind it all.'

'She's just a big bully,' I said. 'And she takes over everything. She just throws her weight around wherever she goes. She has to be at the centre of everything.'

'Bullies usually have difficult lives,' said Mum. 'They are often not very happy people, so they have to take out their bad humour on the people around them.'

'I don't care Mum,' I said. 'I really don't like her.'

'You don't have to like her. You don't have to hang

out with her. You just have to not punch her in the face again!'

Mum laughed. I laughed. Granny laughed.

Charlie put his spoon back into his empty bowl, more noisily than he needed to.

'Mummy, can I punch Aidan in the face?'

☣ ☣ ☣

I turned on my phone as soon as I got back up to my bedroom. Eight new messages. Two from Rebecca, one from Robyn, one from Debbie and one from Amanda, all asking me if I was okay. That was nice of them all. I didn't know that Amanda had my number. I didn't have hers. She obviously knew that, she signed it.

Amanda.

Rebecca and Robyn both said that I only did what lots of people have been wanting to do for years! Debbie just said that she was thinking of me, that she hoped that I was okay.

There was also a message from Evelyn, wishing me good luck in the final, and there was one from Sally to tell me that she and her mum were definitely going to the game, that they would be driving down in the morning. My heart did a little flip. Brilliant! It would be brilliant to see Sally. And there was a video from Sally of a cat falling off a window ledge into a sink.

I replied:

'Thanks Robyn, I'm fine. See you tomorrow.'

'Thanks Rebecca, I'm fine. See you tomorrow.'

I didn't want to get into the whole I-only-did-what-lots-of-people-have-been-wanting-to-do-for-years thing. Not in text messages anyway.

'Thanks very much Amanda. See you tomorrow.'

'Thanks Debbie. Sorry for ruining training on everybody.'

'Thanks Evelyn!'

'That's fantastic Sal! ☺ Come to the house if you're here early enough.'

(I think that it's correct to write you're, even in text messages, not ur or, even worse, your, when you mean you're.)

I had just put on my navy hoodie when I heard the doorbell ring. I looked out the window and saw Stephen's car parked beside our gate.

'Anna!' Mum called from the hall, as I heard her usher the visitors into the sitting room.

I zipped up my hoodie and went down the stairs, one step by one step, slowly, reluctantly. Mum and Stephen and Tina were in the sitting room when I walked in, all standing up, Mum with her back to the fireplace, Stephen and Tina with their backs to the sofa, facing Mum. They were talking about the weather for the following day. It didn't look like it was going to rain for the final.

'Hi, Anna,' said Stephen.

Tina didn't say anything.

'Hi,' I said.

I just stood beside Mum. Stephen said that he didn't want tea. Or coffee. Tina shook her head when Mum asked her if she wanted anything. She kept her head down. She just looked at the floor.

I wondered how this was going to go. Was I going to have to apologise to Tina? I didn't feel like apologising to Tina. Suddenly, Stephen spoke.

'Tina has something that she wants to say.'

He looked at Tina. Tina continued to look at the floor. Her right cheek was a tiny bit red, just below her eye, but otherwise she looked fine. There was silence for a second or two.

'Tina?' Stephen said.

'I'm sorry,' she said.

More silence.

'Sorry for what?' prompted Stephen.

'I'm sorry for calling you names, Mrs Hogan.'

'And what?' said Stephen.

'It's okay,' Mum interrupted.

That was a pity. I was looking forward to hearing what else. In fairness to Mum though, it was fairly painful, and I was doubting the sincerity of it all. It all seemed to be a little bit rehearsed.

'Anna has something to say too, don't you, Anna?'

I did? We hadn't rehearsed anything. I suppose I was sorry too, now that Tina was sorry.

'I'm sorry too,' I said.

It was all very awkward. I didn't think that I was sorry, but I was. I meant it when I said it. I felt sorry. I felt sorry for Tina, and that surprised me. She seemed so meek, so vulnerable, standing there in our house, in the middle of our sitting room, apologising to Mum. And to me I suppose. It was easier to feel sorry, and to say sorry to her, after she had said sorry to me.

'Okay,' said Mum.

'Right,' said Stephen. 'That's all good. Thanks, Anna. Now shake hands.'

I took a step towards Tina and stretched out my right hand. She looked at me from behind her dark hair, which was falling limply down both sides of her face, obscuring most of her face. Her eyes were red. She looked timid. Helpless. Suddenly this surge of pity rushed through my chest. Poor Tina.

She stretched out her hand and I grabbed it. Her handshake was weak. She hardly grabbed my hand at all. It was like shaking a cold lifeless object that was just attached to the end of her arm. I willed her to wrap her fingers around the back of my hand, but she didn't. She just stood there, the weight of the world on her shoulders. Not the Tina who would strut around the school or the pitch, not the Tina who commandeered the dressing room, who answered back, who determined what the mood would be in training, and sometimes even how hard we trained. Not the Tina who would put the fear of God in you if you encountered her in the school yard or in the corridor.

This was a vulnerable little kid standing in front of me. Suddenly, it felt like I was the dominant one. I don't have a little sister, but I imagined that this would be how it would feel if I did. Tina was looking up at me. She wasn't smaller than me, but her shoulders were drooping and her head was down, so she had to look up in order to look into my face. Her big, brown, sad eyes, staring up at me. I felt this urge to hug her, so I did.

I didn't let go of her right hand. I used that to pull her closer to me and, before I knew what I was doing, I had wrapped my left arm around her right shoulder. It felt like the most natural thing in the world. She didn't put her left arm around me, but she didn't resist either, she just allowed me hug her. I could feel the warmth of the side of her head against the side of my head, and I could feel her nose against my shoulder and the warmth of her breath on my neck.

And I could feel her sobbing.

Her whole body felt limp. Like, if I moved away or let go of her, her body would fall in a crumpled pile onto the floor. I didn't let go. Her sobbing got more notice-able and more audible. I just held onto her. Mum and Stephen were still in the room, or I was sure that they were still in the room, but I couldn't see them and I wasn't really aware of their presence. I just kept my chin on Tina's shoulder and my left arm wrapped around her back.

'I'm sorry, Anna,' Tina said suddenly, muffled in my shoulder. She didn't move her head back, she just mumbled through the muffle, and she sniffled. 'I'm so sorry,' she sobbed. 'You're so nice. You've always been nice to me.'

I wasn't sure about that one, but I didn't say anything.

'You've never been mean to me, and I've been so mean to you. And you're a great football player.'

There was silence as Tina sniffled and drew a breath, which, after a few seconds, I felt the urge to break.

'Well, I wouldn't say great.'

Tina laughed through her sobbing. I could feel her laughing into my shoulder. I smiled. Tina drew her head back away from my shoulder. I could see her face clearly now. She was a mess. Her hair was all over the place, her eyes were all puffy and red, the tears were smudged onto her cheek, and the red mark just below her left eye seemed to be a little redder now than I thought it had been earlier.

'Well, good anyway,' smiled Tina through the mess. 'Quite good.'

'I'll settle for quite good.'

Suddenly Stephen was beside us and had his arms around both of us. He beckoned for Mum to join in, but Mum just put her hand up and smiled. She was happy to stay out of it.

Clever Mum.

'This is what we need,' Stephen said. 'The two of you together. Bonding.'

I cringed.

'If you can bond like this on the football pitch tomorrow, those Glendore girls don't stand a chance.'

• • • • • • •

Chapter 26

FINAL DAY

I didn't sleep very well on Saturday night. I tossed and turned and woke up and half-slept and dreamt. Weird dreams. I dreamt about the match. The final. We were wearing these strange pink shirts, and Sally was on our team, and the girl who boxed Debbie in the semi-final was on our team. The Ardart girl. On our team. And Tina passed to me lots and encouraged me. And Daddy was there.

I woke up before the final whistle, so I don't know if we won or lost. Or I'm not sure if it was before the final whistle or not, because the dream kind of fizzled out, or morphed into a different dream, about me and

Miss Ferguson sitting in a classroom, just the two of us, and she explaining the meanings of weird words to me, words I had never heard before. Like 'equizicle'. She made a point of telling me that it was 'i-c-l-e,' not 'a-c-l-e.' I couldn't remember what she told me it meant, and I don't think that it's even a word.

Dreams are crazy.

I woke up sad though. Daddy hadn't been behind the goals in my dream. He had been on the sideline, beside Stephen and Mum, beside the dugout. Every time I looked over at him, he was smiling. I just wanted to go over to him and give him a hug, but the game was on, I was in the middle of a final, so I couldn't. I figured that I'd hug him at half-time or after the final whistle had blown, but we never got to half-time or to full-time.

I had this feeling that I should go over and hug him during the game, that I should seize the opportunity, because he was there. But I knew that I couldn't, not during a game. I also had this feeling that it wasn't real. He wasn't behind the goals, which I thought was weird. And the pink shirts.

Sometimes when you are in a dream, you know that you are in a dream. It still didn't mean that I wasn't sad when I woke up though. It still didn't mean that I didn't cry. Well kind of cry. I don't know if it counts as crying when your eyes well up, but you cop yourself on before any tears spill over onto your cheeks.

It still didn't mean that I didn't miss Daddy more than anything in the world.

Today of all days. Final day. County final day. He would have loved this. He would have been up early and he would have got me breakfast and he would have made a big fuss of me. We probably would have gone for a walk early in the morning and talked about the game and how it might go and what I might do. He would have made sure that I relaxed. He had this way of making football seem important enough to make you want to do well, but trivial enough to make you feel not nervous about it.

Do your best. That's all you can do.

Not that Mum didn't make a fuss of me. She did. She was up early and she had the breakfast on. I could smell the bacon from the hall before I got into the kitchen. Mum and Granny and Grandad were all there when I got there. They all beamed when I opened the door and walked in.

'Morning, pet,' said Mum. All smiles.

'All set?'

I went to speak, I wanted to say yes and smile, but I just burst into tears.

'Aw, pet.'

Mum had me smothered in her dressing gown before I knew what was happening. I wanted to stay there. She smelled like sleep. I didn't want to let go. I cried some more there.

'It's not fair,' I said.

'I know it's not, pet. It's not fair at all.'

There was cry in her voice too.

I didn't speak for a little while. I'd say for about a minute or a minute and a half. It was just me and Mum and Mum's dressing gown, standing in the kitchen. Mum stood there for as long as I wanted her to. I'd say that she would have stood there all day if I had wanted her to. But we had a final to play.

Eventually, I pushed myself away and looked at her face. She had been crying all right.

'You okay?' she asked me.

I nodded.

'So, are you all set?!'

We laughed.

I went over to Granny and gave her a hug. She had been crying too.

'Morning, Granny.'

And to Grandad. I wasn't sure if he had been crying. I had never seen Grandad crying, but he looked a little welled up.

'Morning, Grandad.'

Breakfast was good. Orange juice and brown bread and a poached egg and sausages and rashers. I know that porridge is good for you, and porridge Monday to Friday is fine, but a few sausages and rashers on Sunday, on Final Day, was a real treat.

'Brenda called earlier,' Mum said. 'She and Sally are on the way, but they're not going to come here first. They're going to go straight to Ballinakill.'

That was probably best. I wanted to see Sally and all, but she would have been a distraction on the morning of the final. I wouldn't have been able to give her the attention that she would want, or the attention that I would want to give her. I was happy that they weren't coming to the house. I was happy that they were coming to the match though. I was really happy about that. I would see them later.

I had never played in Ballinakill before. I had never been to a match in Ballinakill before. It was a big deal though, to play in Ballinakill. A county final. We were meeting at the club and we were all going on a bus together to Ballinakill. That was a big deal too.

I looked at the clock on the wall. Five past nine. Fifty-five minutes before the bus was leaving from the club. Nice time. Not too long, and still no rush. I put the last piece of bacon into my mouth and finished my orange juice.

'You go and get ready now pet,' said Mum. 'I'll clean up here.'

'Thanks Mum.'

I ran upstairs and into my room. I pulled on my tracksuit bottoms and my t-shirt and my tracksuit top, and I got my gear bag out. Black shorts, green socks, gloves, towel, gum shield, orange socks.

Wait. No orange socks.

Where were my orange socks?

'Mum, where are my orange socks?' I shouted out loud into my drawer as I rummaged through it.

They weren't there. They weren't in my football socks and shorts drawer. They weren't at the side and they weren't at the back.

I closed the drawer. No need to panic. I opened my sports jerseys drawer. Mum probably put them in there by mistake. They weren't on top of my jerseys. I rummaged around a little. They weren't under my Nike t-shirt and they weren't under my Cúl Camp jersey.

This was getting serious.

'Mum!'

I closed that drawer and opened my normal socks

and underwear drawer. You would see them quickly if they were there, luminous orange socks in among mainly white and pink and pale-coloured socks and underwear. They weren't obviously there, so I rummaged around again. No socks.

'Mum!'

I opened my wardrobe and pushed some clothes around. Now it was time to panic. My orange socks weren't anywhere.

'Mum!'

Mum was on the landing on her way into my room when I opened by bedroom door. We nearly bumped into each other.

'I can't find my orange socks Mum.'

I was nearly crying, more with frustration than with sadness.

'Don't worry pet,' Mum said calmly. 'We'll find them. When did you have them last?'

'I wore them for the Ardart game,' I said. 'The semi-final. I haven't worn them since then. I put them in the wash then. They should have been with my gear from that game. My black shorts and my green socks. Remember? They were on my bed the other night?'

'Did you not wear your green socks in that game?'

'Mum! I did. But I wore my orange socks under

them. Remember?

'Oh yes, I remember now.'

Was she doing this on purpose?

'And where are your green socks?'

'I have them. You left them on my bed, remember? I have them in my bag.'

I just stood there, expectantly. Expecting Mum to solve this, to produce my orange socks. To tell me that she had them. She looked thoughtful.

'You know,' she said. 'I think I took your orange socks out of that wash. I think that I was washing something else in that wash, and I was afraid that the colour from the orange socks would run. They're a very deep orange, aren't they?'

'Where are they Mum?!'

'I may not have washed them. They may still be in the laundry.'

'Ah Mum!'

It didn't matter. I could wear them again, even if they hadn't been washed.

'So are they in the laundry now?' I asked.

'Probably.'

I ran into the bathroom, to the laundry basket. They would be down at the bottom then if they were in it. I dug deep into the dirty laundry – it was gross – but no sign. I emptied the contents of the basked onto the bathroom floor – even grosser – but still no sign.

Mum had been watching me all this time from the bathroom door. I looked up at her, on my knees on the bathroom floor, exasperated. I had that Mum-do-something feeling in my stomach.

'Hold on,' said Mum, and she disappeared down the stairs.

Slowly I picked myself up and I picked up the dirty laundry and I put it back into the basket. I felt exhausted and panicked at the same time. I needed my orange socks. I needed the link to Daddy. I needed the comfort and the confidence that Daddy's orange socks gave me, that Daddy gave me through his orange socks.

I went back into my room and looked through all the drawers again. I checked behind the wardrobe, behind my drawers, under my bed, behind the headboard, even under the duvet and under my pillow. Still no sign.

Mum came back in through my open bedroom door. She had nothing in her hands. No socks.

'I can't find them pet.'

My heart sank. I felt like crying, but I didn't. I was frustrated and angry. Frustrated at myself and angry at Mum. Why couldn't she just have washed my orange socks in the normal wash? And why didn't I go and get my gear together last night? At least then I would have had time to turn the house upside down. I would have stayed up all night to look for them if that was what it would have taken. My orange socks had to be some-where.

'Look pet,' said Mum. 'It's five to 10. The bus is leav-ing in five minutes. You're late even as it is. I'll drop you down to the bus, then I'll come back here and I'll find them. Then I'll bring them to you in Ballinakill. The match doesn't start until 12, so we have time.'

She was right. I had to go. Without my socks. And we did have time. Mum could find them. She didn't need me to help her find them. I wasn't happy though. I needed to know that I had my socks.

I looked Mum in the eye and bit my tongue.

'Please find them Mum.'

Chapter 27

• • • • • •

FINAL PREPARATIONS

The bus journey to Ballinakill was not enjoyable. There was a nervousness about the place. Stephen was obviously nervous, Patrick was obviously nervous, and everybody felt it.

The noisy ones were quiet and the quiet ones were noisy. Sue was talking loudly on the bus when I got on. Sue never spoke. She was always quiet. And Tina was quiet, which was completely out of character for her. She wasn't saying a word. Maybe she had said all that she wanted to say before I arrived. Everyone was on the bus when I arrived. I was last to arrive. Again.

I hated that, getting on the bus with everybody on it.

And it was even worse now than it usually would be. Just two days after the training ground incident. Two days after I had punched Tina in the face.

I wondered if some of the girls' opinions of me had changed since the incident. Because of the incident. Punch-gate. This was the first time since then that I had seen everybody. Well, everybody except Tina.

Did they like me less? Did they think that I was a big bully? Did they think that I had got above myself? Who was I, this new person into the team, into the parish, punching poor Tina, whose family had probably lived in Ballymarra for generations? Were they afraid of me? God, I hoped they weren't afraid of me.

And everyone had paired off. Obviously. Sofia was beside Aoife. Debbie and Lily were together, in the second seat from the front. They both said 'Hi, Anna' when I walked past them. Ciara and Sandra were beside each other, they were talking to each other as I walked past them. They didn't stop to say hello. Maybe they hadn't noticed me. Maybe they were engrossed in their conversation.

Orla and Shauna were together. Shauna said 'Hi, Anna', and Orla stretched out her hand and gave me a semi-high-five. Robyn and Rebecca were sitting together, of course. They both smiled.

Tina was sitting beside Sinéad, as usual, in the second last seat on the left, Tina by the window, Sinéad at the aisle, with Edel sitting in front of them, on her own, turned around in her seat to talk to them. They had paired off in a threesome, as they always did. Nobody slagged me for being late. I kind of wished they had. That would have been easier.

Patrick was sitting beside Stephen and Orla's mum was sitting beside Sandra's mum.

My options were, sit on my own in the third last seat on the right, or sit beside Edel, in front of Tina and Sinéad – and there was no way that I was going to do that – or sit beside Amanda.

'Hi Amanda,' I said. 'Anyone here?'

'No, not at all.'

Amanda said 'not at all' a lot.

She picked up her tracksuit top from the seat beside her and put it on her knee. I got the impression that she wasn't certain whether or not she wanted anybody to sit beside her, or whether or not she wanted me to sit beside her, but I sat down anyway. It was the least bad option.

Amanda started to talk just as the bus pulled out from Ballymarra, and she didn't stop talking until we turned off the N11. I'd say I knew more about Amanda by the time we reached the outskirts of Arklow than I knew about my brother Charlie. I knew that she preferred hockey to football, for starters, which was disappointing. I knew that she had no brothers and two sisters, both older, both annoying. I knew that her dad worked in an office in Dublin and was away a lot, and that her mum was at home. And I knew that she fancied some guy named Simon, who went to school in Dublin. I also knew that she was nervous about the match. I knew that before she told me.

Maybe she was wary of me because I had boxed Tina on Friday. Maybe that was making her extra nervous. I don't know. She didn't mention it and I certainly wasn't going to bring it up. Imagine.

'So, what did you think of me boxing Tina on Friday?'

I told Amanda very little about me. She didn't ask and I didn't really want to get into talking about me. I didn't really have much of an opportunity but it suited me not to talk. I was nervous about the game too, and I was nervous about my socks. That aside, I never knew that Amanda had so many words inside her.

Amanda got quieter after Arklow and, as we winded the final winds to Ballinakill, her patter slowed to silence. Actually, the whole bus was silent when the bus stopped at the pitch. It was eerie.

We all filed off the bus and made our way into the dressing room. I quickly scoured the place for Mum's car, but no sign of it. That would have been too good. She was never going to be able to find my socks and beat the bus to Ballinakill.

It was eerie in the dressing room too initially. Tina was normally the one who would make most of the noise, and others would join in around her, but Tina was quiet and I suppose that set the tone for everyone else.

I ended up beside Amanda in the dressing room too, and beside Robyn and one away from Rebecca. I suppose it shouldn't be surprising that, even though we were in a different dressing room, people should gravitate towards the same places. The two dressing rooms were more or less the same shape: rectangular. There aren't too many different variations of rectangular.

There was some murmuring as we got changed, but it was still all very quiet. I resigned myself to the fact that I was going to have to put on my green socks for starters, and that hopefully Mum would arrive with my orange socks before the game started. Left sock first, then right sock. Left boot next, then right boot.

There was a knock on the door and Sandra's mum poked her head in.

'Everybody decent?'

Nobody really answered. She could surely see that everybody was. She held the door open and Stephen and Patrick came in.

'Ah come on, girls,' Stephen said. 'It's like a morgue in here!'

He was right. We were very quiet, and that was not a good thing. It meant that people were nervous, and nervousness can paralyse. We needed to loosen up, we needed to be loose enough to play our game.

'First things first,' said Stephen. 'There was an incident at training on Friday evening, an incident of which I am sure you are all aware.'

The elephant in the room.

My heart did a little jump, and not in a good way. I looked down at the ground. I focused on a little piece of paper that was on the floor, about three feet from where my left foot was, and I fixed my gaze. I didn't blink, I didn't move. I just kept my head down and hoped that this part of the talk would end quickly.

'That has all been sorted now,' said Stephen. 'The people involved have spoken, and everybody is good now. So we're putting that all behind us and moving on.'

Silence.

'Okay?'

There was a muttering of okay around the room. I didn't speak of course. It wasn't my place to be okay or not okay with me punching Tina in the face. I just hoped that everybody else would be okay.

'Right,' said Stephen. This was when Stephen was at his best, at his most authoritative. In the dressing room before a match. He was in full control, he knew what he was saying and he knew what he wanted to say. So competent, so confident. A different person to the one who appeared in our kitchen or in our sitting room from time to time.

'So we'll announce the team that is starting, and then we'll have a chat about it.'

I relaxed, I blinked, I looked away from the little piece of paper on the ground. That was that. That part was over. Stephen was right to address it. I was glad that he had. It was done. It was over.

'Now, before I announce it, this is the team that Patrick and I have decided is the correct team to start today. It doesn't mean that these are our best fifteen players, it just means that this is the team with which we want to start, based on the day, the game, the opposition. And there will be changes during the game, that's for sure. So, if you are not on the first fifteen, don't worry, you may be coming on later. You may get your chance, so stay ready.'

Now I was nervous. What if I wasn't starting? I knew that feeling, expecting to start and not starting. I didn't have my socks yet, so maybe it wouldn't be a bad thing if I wasn't starting. Maybe I wasn't good enough anyway. But I wanted to start. But if I didn't start, the pressure would be off. I wouldn't have these butterflies in my stomach. But I wanted to start. I desperately wanted to start.

There were no major surprises among the backs. Sofia in goals of course. Full-back line, Rebecca, Robyn, Edel. Half-back line, Sandra, Shauna, Orla. Midfield, Lily and Tina. Stephen threw the number eight jersey to Tina and the number nine jersey to Lily. It didn't really matter. They were both midfield.

'Hey, Lily,' called Tina, loudly enough so that Stephen stopped before naming the half-forwards. Tina threw the number eight jersey to Lily and beckoned to her with her hand. Lily looked at her, slightly confused. She stood there for a second or two, with the number eight jersey, the one that she had just caught, in her left hand and the number nine jersey in her right hand.

'What's going on?' asked Stephen.

'Lily has my jersey,' said Tina.

'You just threw it to her,' said Stephen.

'I'm number nine. Everybody knows that.'

It looked like the old Tina had returned. Who is everybody? Everybody in the dressing room? Everybody in Ballymarra? Everybody in the world?

There was silence for a second or two as people looked at Lily. Mild tension. I thought that Stephen would say something like, ah come on Tina, for God's sake. It doesn't matter. But he didn't.

Strangely, I fully understood where Tina was coming from. It *did* matter. She always wore number nine, she wanted to wear number nine in the final. Surely Stephen knew that she was always number nine. It was a mistake to give her number eight. It may have seemed like a tiny thing, but I fully understood that it was probably a really big thing for Tina.

Even so, it was all in Lily's hands. She had possession of both jerseys, she had 90 per cent of the law on her side. While I understood Tina's frame of mind, there was a small part of me that would have liked to have seen Lily throw the number eight jersey back to Tina. Just to see what would happen. How she would react. How Stephen would react.

Lily threw the number nine jersey to Tina. Fair play to Lily. She saw the big picture. It wouldn't have been the ideal preparation for a final, the two midfielders arguing over who would wear number eight and who would wear number nine. Maybe Lily wanted to wear number eight anyway. That was her jersey. Maybe she wanted to wear number eight as much as Tina wanted to wear number nine.

Tina didn't say thanks. She just caught the jersey and sat down. She didn't start to put it on. She knew people were looking at her. She only had returned to her what was rightfully hers in the first place, so why should she even say thanks? The old Tina was back all right.

'Debbie, number 10,' Stephen said slowly. 'Right half-forward.'

Now I was getting nervous. I wanted to be number 12. I really wanted to start on the left wing. The left corner would be second choice, but the left wing was where I really wanted to be.

'Sinéad, centre half-forward. On the forty.'

Stephen threw the number 11 jersey to Sinéad, and I held my breath.

'Left wing,' Stephen said, as he held the number 12 jersey in his cocked right hand, ready to throw it when he laid eyes on his intended recipient. I almost put up my hand even before his eyes alighted on me.

'Anna,' he said, as he threw the jersey to me.

I felt a swell of relief and pride and excitement and nervousness all at the same time. Brilliant. I was starting on the left wing. And Debbie was on the right. I looked over and caught Debbie smiling at me.

'Shelley, right corner,' said Stephen.

'On the square, Amanda,' as he threw number 14 to Amanda beside me.

'And number 15,' said Stephen, 'is Aoife.'

The hum around the dressing room started to get louder as Stephen threw the remaining jerseys to the subs, one by one. I was glad that Aoife was on. I felt bad that she seemed to lose her place on the starting 15 when I arrived. And, to be honest, while I felt bad for Ciara, who was obviously disappointed when Stephen threw the number 17 jersey to her, I thought that there wasn't much between Ciara and Aoife in terms of ability.

And Aoife had this knack of nicking a goal. She had that in her favour. And she had been playing well in training. Not that it was my place to have an opinion on it, but I thought that Stephen was right to start Aoife in front of Ciara.

'Right, settle down,' said Stephen, and the hum started to quieten down again.

* * * * * *

Chapter 28

FIRST-HALF PAIN

Stephen's team talk was brilliant. The best he had ever given, I'd say. He struck the right balance between impressing upon us the importance of this game, the history that went with it, and the fact that it was just another game. Just like the semi-final and the quarter-final, which we won.

Everyone was fired up. I left the dressing room wanting to get out and play, but also wanting my socks.

I looked towards the goals to the left of the dressing room, but there was no shadow there. I looked towards the goals to the right, no shadow there either. Then I checked both sidelines, but no shadow, and no sign of Mum.

The Glendore girls were already out on the pitch, kicking into the goals to the left, so I was just heading with the girls to the right-hand goals when I heard somebody calling me.

'Anna! Anna!'

I looked over to my right, and there was Sally, jumping up and down, with her mum trying to restrain her. I ran over to her and she almost jumped on top of me!

'Hi, how are you, you look fab, brilliant, how are you feeling …'

She squeaked it all out in her high-pitched excited-to-the-point-of-exploding voice! It was brilliant to see her. I missed Sally so much.

Sally Cat.

'Sally, brilliant, I'm great. Thanks so much for coming. You're crazy!'

Brenda leaned over and gave me a hug too.

'Good luck, Anna,' little Alan said.

I gave him a hug too. He was getting tall. He may have been Sally's annoying little brother, but it was still great to see him.

'Best of luck, Anna,' Brenda said. 'We'll be cheering. Where's your mum?'

'She'll be here soon,' I said, as I wondered the same

thing.

The stretching had already started by the time I got over to the girls. Then the pre-match drills. Hand-pass, move, catch, hand-pass, move, join the back of the line. It was fast and accurate. Everybody was moving well.

'Right, kick-passes,' shouted Patrick.

Kick-pass, move. Catch, solo, kick-pass, move. I liked this one. A couple of balls went a little astray. Sandra's pass went over my head, so I had to go and retrieve it, and I had to stretch for Rebecca's, but it wasn't bad. It was sharp and it was fast, and everyone was tuned in.

'Anna!'

Patrick was calling me.

'And Debbie. Come here for a second. Both of you.'

I got over to Patrick before Debbie did.

'You two, you are two of the most skilful players on the team.'

I was a bit embarrassed, but also delighted that Patrick should say that. I tried to maintain the same facial expression. I hoped that my inner smile of pride was not showing on my face.

'All the things we worked on,' Patrick said. 'The passing, the movement, the interlinking, the switching. Are you both comfortable with all of that?'

We both nodded.

'Use your instincts. You are both instinctive players. Trust your instinct. Trust your own judgement. And if it doesn't happen initially, don't worry. It will happen later. Just keep at it. We know that it works. Okay?'

We both nodded again.

'Debbie, you're starting on the right, right? Number 10?'

Debbie nodded.

'Anna, you're starting on the left. So that they won't expect that you are going to switch. But switch when you want. Just do it. Go with it when it feels right. You know each other's game well enough by now. Okay?'

'Okay!'

We said it in unison. Debbie put her two be-gloved hands up in the air, and I touched them with my two bare hands. We smiled. We can do this.

I looked towards the left-hand goals, but no shadow. I looked towards the right-hand goals, but no shadow. I looked towards the dugout, but no Mum.

I was getting fairly frantic now. Where was the shadow? Where was Daddy now, for the final, when I needed him most? And where was Mum with my socks? I needed my socks. I needed Daddy.

Stephen was calling us all in, towards the dugout. Tina was coming over from the centre of the pitch, away from the referee and the Glendore number six, where she had probably just been for the coin toss.

'Okay come in girls. Get a drink.'

I fell into step with Tina as we all converged on the dug-out.

'All set?' I said to her.

It was the first time I had spoken to her since she had been our house. I wanted to say something to her before the game started. I was glad to have this opportunity.

She looked back at me and blinked. A big blink. If I hadn't known Tina, I would have said that there was fear in her eyes.

'Eh, yeah. I guess.'

And she moved to her left, away from me. I hadn't expected that reaction. I hadn't expected that we would be best buddies, but I thought at least that we would talk to each other. Maybe she was embarrassed, because she had broken down and cried in our house. Maybe she was afraid of me now, because I had punched her. I really hoped that she wasn't afraid of me. I doubted she was. I hoped that she was just embarrassed. Or just uninterested.

I looked beyond the dugout as we approached it, but still there was no sign of Mum. I scoured the sideline.

I saw Sally and Brenda and Alan, and I saw Debbie's mum and dad, and I saw Tina's mum, but I couldn't find Mum.

We got to the dugout and we all gathered around Stephen.

'Right,' said Stephen. 'This is it. We've done all the talking. It's all down to you girls now. The fifteen who start and the subs who will come on. It comes down to this. Just play to your potential. You know that you are good enough.'

As he spoke, I looked down towards the goals in front of us again, but there was no shadow there. I glanced behind me to the goals behind us. No shadow. I closed my eyes and tried to picture Daddy.

Ready. Focus on the pitch. Focus on the game. Take responsibility. Do your best.

It wasn't easy. I was finding it difficult to picture Daddy. I could see his body, lean and slim and tall, I could picture him in his jeans and in his dark blue shirt, but I was finding it difficult to fill in the details of his face. I was also finding it difficult to get my head tuned into the game, to block out other things around me. I wondered if Sally was okay. She and Alan and Brenda had travelled a long way. Were they hungry or had they stopped for something to eat on the way? And were

Debbie's parents nervous about her playing, after her injury? And had Mum found my orange socks? And where was she?!

'Who are we?' Tina was saying.

Everybody had their arms around each other and everybody had said 'Ballymarra!' before I had tuned back in.

I put my left arm around Shauna and my right arm around Robyn.

'Who are we?' Tina shouted again.

'Ballymarra!' everyone shouted, including me.

'Who are we?' Tina shouted at the top of her voice.

'Ballymarra! Ballymarra! Ballymarra!'

Tina had probably won the toss, I thought, as we were playing into the left-hand goals in the first half, with the slight breeze. Stephen always maintained that, if you had the choice, you played with the wind in the first half. That it was better to try to build up an advantage than to be chasing the game, and because the wind could drop or change direction for the second half.

As I took my place at left half-forward and put my mouth guard into my mouth, I glanced more hopefully than expectantly behind the goals into which we were shooting, but no shadow. I glanced up behind Sofia's goals, and no shadow. I looked at our dug-out, and no

Mum. I looked around the sideline, around both side-lines, and no Mum.

The Glendore number five extended her hand, so I shook it. That was very nice of her, I thought.

'Best of luck,' she said in an unexpectedly deep voice.

'You too,' I said.

I turned to face the centre of the pitch, where the referee was throwing the ball in between Tina and Lily and the two Glendore midfielders, and I felt this impact on my left shoulder. It caught me unawares, it nearly knocked me over. I looked to my left, and there was the Glendore number five, the girl who had just shook my hand and wished me luck, after hitting me a shoulder, full-on, shoulder to shoulder. The ref obviously didn't see it. He couldn't have. He was busy throwing the ball in. I tried to look her in the face, but she was looking straight ahead, battle-face on.

I felt weak, helpless. I didn't have my socks and I didn't have Daddy, and I didn't even have Mum at the game. And here was this strange girl shaking my hand and hitting me shoulders.

Glendore won the throw-in and were moving up the field. They put a few passes together and their number 11 shot, but the ball went wide. Good. I moved to my right, towards the sideline as Sofia prepared to take the kick-out.

Lily won the kick-out and turned to her left. Debbie got free of her marker and moved to her right, towards the centre, and Lily found her with an accurate pass. I cut inside to my left and called for the ball.

'Debbie!'

Debbie saw me and passed quickly with the outside of her left foot. It wasn't a perfect pass, but it wasn't bad, it was in my stride and I could get it. The ball bounced once in front of me and I stretched to collect it but, as I did, I felt an arm on my back and another arm in front of me, punching my left arm and punching the ball away from me. I got my right fingertips to it, but the punch took it out of my reach. The Glendore number six collected it easily and cleared.

'Unlucky, Anna,' I heard Stephen shout.

'Well done, Lily, well done, Debbie. Next one, Anna.'

But the next one was worse. Sinéad played a perfect pass to me. I collected it in my chest all right but, when I went to pass to Debbie, it got away from me a bit and my marker was able to get a hand in to knock it away.

My marker stayed tight to me the whole time, and I hated that.

I switched with Debbie after about seven or eight minutes, I went on the right and she went on the left, and I thought that my marker, the Glendore number five, the right half-back, might stay on their right and mark Debbie, but she didn't. She stayed with me, she followed me over to our right, her left, and she stuck with me, like a limpet. She stuck with me wherever I went. If I had gone into the dressing room to go to the toilet, I'm sure she would have come with me. In fairness, if I had been the Glendore manager, I wouldn't have taken her off me either. She was getting the better of me.

Where was Mum?

Nothing went right. My passing was off, my shooting was off, my timing was off. One of their kick-outs came my way, but their number five caught it over my head and I ended up lying on my back on the ground. I had a shot blocked down from inside the 21 that I really should have scored, I was smothered once and the ref gave a free against me, and I kicked one ball, intended for Aoife, out over the sideline.

It was a disaster. When that ball went out over the sideline, I looked towards the goal. I squinted a little, I closed my right eye, I closed my left eye, but there was no shadow.

Where are you Daddy?

Once I was in, or I could have been in. I had lost the

number five for once, and Shelley had the ball on the left hand side. She tried to get it over to me and, if she had, I would only have had the goalkeeper to beat. I may have missed anyway, the way that I was playing, but it never got to me. Shelley's hand-pass was weak and their number two was able to collect it over her head and pass it to their number seven.

I had just one other shot on goal. I should have scored too. I got clear and Debbie played a lovely pass to me. Right into my chest. I was about 25 metres from goal, just a little to the right, and I had a free shot. It was a more than scorable opportunity. I started the ball out a little to the right, right-footed, and tried to curl it in. But it curled too much. I didn't start it out far enough to the right, and it curled wide on the left. Just wide, but wide. They all register the same on the scoreboard: zero.

When the half-time whistle went, I felt deflated, frustrated. We were behind, six points to four, and I hadn't contributed. I had been a liability.

I dragged my heels towards the dug-out. I didn't want to face anybody. I knew that Stephen would encourage me, I knew that some of the girls would encourage me, but I also knew that I had been poor. And still no sign of Mum.

'Come on in, girls,' Stephen was saying. 'Look, we're still in this. Things just didn't go right for us in the first half. We shouldn't be two points behind. If we had taken some of those chances, we would be level or in front.'

Two of them were mine. At least two of them.

'Sofia, keep your kick-outs away from that tall girl, the number eight. She's winning everything in the middle. Look for Sandra on the right or Orla on the left.'

Sofia nodded.

'Shauna, don't be afraid to carry the ball more out of defence. You have the skill. Down the centre. There is space there.'

Shauna nodded.

'Tina and Lily in midfield, you need to be stronger. You need to be tougher. Those two Glendore girls are running everything from midfield. You need to get in their faces.'

I couldn't see Lily's face, she was obscured by Rebecca's head, but I could see Tina's face, and her mouth curled up into a little snarl. She didn't nod.

'Sinéad, you're doing great,' said Stephen. 'More of the same in the second half. Your scores kept us in it in the first half. Just keep doing what you're doing. And Debbie, stay on the right. Don't switch to the left.

You're doing better on the right.'

No more switching for us then. I was staying on the left.

'Shelley and Aoife, stay forward. Stay in the corners. Don't be sucked into coming out the field. Start off in the corners, almost on the end line, and move out from there when you need to. But the end line is your starting point. Okay?'

Shelley and Aoife both nodded.

'Come on girls. We're better than this. We're better than them. We're better than we showed in the first half. We know that we are. We just need to go and do it in the second half.'

Nothing for me. No advice, no change. That was unusual, but I got it. I was so awful. He knew that I knew that I was awful. He didn't need to say anything to me.

'Anna!'

Mum's voice. It was brilliant to hear Mum's voice.

'I'm so sorry. It took me so long to find them.'

She was holding my orange socks. Holding them out to me.

'And then the traffic coming into Ballinakill …'

'It's okay, Mum,' I said quickly. 'Thanks Mum. It's great. You're great. You got them.'

I was sitting on the ground taking off my boots before I finished speaking. Mum crouched down on her hunkers beside me.

'I'm so sorry for everything, Anna. I know how much the socks mean to you. I've been thinking about it a lot. You have a lot of time to think when you drive to Ballinakill! I know that they're a link to Dad for you …'

'It's okay, Mum,' I interrupted again. 'Honestly. It's great that you got them. Thanks so much. And it's brilliant that you're here.'

She smiled and just stayed there on her hunkers beside me as I took off my green socks and put on my orange socks, left foot first, right foot second. I paused for a second. It felt so good to get my orange socks on my feet. They fit perfectly, they felt so comfortable, but it wasn't just that. It felt like they belonged. That there had been something lacking, and now it wasn't lacking any more.

I put my green socks on over my orange socks, left foot first, right foot second, and then my boots. Left boot first, right boot second. I tied my laces and stood up. Mum stood up beside me, still smiling. I felt good. Comfortable. Confident. Ready for anything.

'Anna.'

Stephen's voice came from behind me.

'I'm going to take you off.'

I had to do a double-take. Did he say that he was going to take me off? Like, now? Before the second half had even started?

'I'm sorry, Anna,' he continued. 'It's just not happening for you today. You're just not at the races.'

I felt like crying. Now? Just when I had got my orange socks? This was terrible. I wasn't even getting a chance.

'I'm sorry, Emma,' Stephen was saying to Mum, as if he had just realised that Mum was there.

'Ah, Stephen,' said Mum. 'Give her ten more minutes.'

'I've already decided Emma,' Stephen said. 'I've already told Ciara to warm up.'

'Come on Stephen. Ciara can warm up and go on in ten minutes. And I've just arrived.'

'Emma, I can't allow my decisions in a county final to be governed by whether or not you can get to the game on time.'

Mum just looked at him. She looked hurt and angry. This was a side to Stephen that I hadn't seen before. It was fairly mean. Mum had broken up with him all right.

'And Anna is affecting Tina,' Stephen continued with

a new-found confidence. 'Tina just told me that Anna's poor play is affecting her game too.'

Mum looked at him, incredulously. I couldn't believe it either. That my poor play was causing Tina to play poorly? Really?

'Seriously Stephen?' Mum said, saying exactly what I was thinking.

Stephen looked a little embarrassed. As if he had said too much.

'You can give her ten minutes Stephen,' Mum said in that slow, deliberate voice that she uses when she is angry but is trying not to show her anger. I sensed that she was getting the upper hand though with this one. That Stephen's Tina comment had given her the upper hand.

'You said that it's not happening for Anna. It might happen for her in the second half. She's a good player. Give her a chance to show that. That's what a good manager would do.'

Stephen looked at Mum for a second. He wasn't happy.

'Ten minutes,' he said eventually. 'Not a minute longer.'

* * * * * *

Chapter 29

FINAL WHISTLE

'Who are we?'

'Ballymarra!'

'Who are we?'

'Ballymarra!'

'Who are we?'

'Ballymarra! Ballymarra! Ballymarra!'

We broke from our huddle and I went to take up my place at left half-forward. Second half, we were shooting into the other goals. I felt good. Comfortable in my gear, comfortable in my socks and boots, no pain, no injury, not even a little niggle. I looked to my left and saw the Glendore girls still in their huddle. I resisted the urge to look to my right, down towards the goals until I could resist it no longer. I glanced up as I jogged towards the far side of the pitch, and I held my breath.

There it was. The shadow. My shadow. Daddy. If it was Daddy. My heart did a little flip and I smiled involuntarily and let out a little gasp.

'Daddy,' I whispered out loud.

He was as he always was when he appeared. Barely decipherable, just about distinguishable, but there, definitely there, and smiling. I couldn't see the features of his face. I wished that I could see the features of his face. But I could tell that he was smiling. I couldn't really make out where the shadow ended, the edges were blurred into the sky behind, but I could see his body, and I could see his arms. He was just there, almost motionless, but definitely smiling.

I got to my position on the left side of the field, on my own, and I closed my eyes.

'Are you ready?' I thought.

'I am,' I said out loud.

'Tuned in?' I said in my head.

'Tuned in,' I said out loud.

'Concentrate on what is happening on the pitch,' I thought. 'Take responsibility. Do your best.'

'Okay,' I said out loud.

I kept my eyes closed. My mind was clear. I imagined Daddy putting his hands on my head and kissing me on the forehead.

I felt good, not sad. I felt reassured, comforted. Not lonely.

By the time I opened my eyes, the Glendore girls were on the pitch, my number five beside me again.

The referee blew his whistle and threw the ball up between the four midfielders. As he did, I could see out of the corner of my eye the Glendore number five's right shoulder coming for my left shoulder. Just in time, I braced myself. She hit me all right, and the shoulder moved me sideways, but she felt the impact as much as I did. She moved back to her left as much as I moved to my right, and I felt no pain. No free kick, but no pain either. I suppose the ref can't see everything.

Lily almost won the throw-in cleanly, but the Glendore number nine knocked the ball out of her hands just before she had it fully in her grasp. It bounced once, twice, and Tina was on it. She took the ball into her chest and moved forward. As she did, I braced myself and hit my marker's right shoulder with my left shoulder. It was a good shoulder, it caught her square. I put the full weight of my body behind it, so much so that if she had managed to avoid me, I would have probably ended up flying through the air and landing on the ground. But she didn't. Not even a little bit. She wasn't expecting it, she wasn't braced for the collision, and it rocked her. She didn't fall, but she almost did, and it had enough of an impact to give me a head start on her.

'Tina!' I called as I cut inside and moved forward on the left.

Tina soloed the ball once and looked up. Then she hopped it and moved forward a little bit more. I thought that she had taken too long on the ball, she was being closed down by the Glendore number eight, but she released it just on time. The ball sailed over the heads of Sinéad and the Glendore number six, and towards me.

I wasn't panicked, I felt at ease. My first ball in the second half, after a horrendous first half, but I didn't feel under pressure. The ball skidded a little as it bounced, it ran away from me a bit, but I stretched out my left hand and just reached it. I took it into my chest without breaking stride and soloed once.

I had the time to assess the situation in front of me. It's remarkable how, when you relax in a game, you can think clearly and you seem to have the time that you need in order to make the right decision. Shelley was to my right, but she was marked. Aoife was to my left, but she was behind me, and she was marked anyway.

Amanda was in front of me, and she and her marker were blocking my path to goal.

The 21 wasn't that far in front of me, and the goals beyond that line, almost straight ahead, looked inviting. I took the time to steady myself and I shot. Straight on. I connected with the ball exactly as I wanted to connect with the ball. Straight, with the top of my foot, close to my toes.

As soon as I hit it, I knew that it was good. It didn't go too high, but it didn't need to. It was a good, strong, shot, straight on, not curling, heading purposefully towards the goals, high enough and strong enough to clear the crossbar. And it did. It went straight over the black spot.

As it did, I had a look behind the goals, and there was the shadow. He was just standing there, a hazy shadow, just about make-out-able, but his arms were out in front and his shoulders moving, as if his hands were clapping. And still smiling. Definitely smiling. I still couldn't make out the features of his face, but I was sure that he was smiling, and that made me smile.

'Great score, Anna!' Debbie said from behind me. I smiled at her and I turned and made my way back towards the left-hand side of the field. As I did, I caught Tina's eye, and I gave her a thumbs-up sign.

'Great pass, Tina.'

I turned around to face the kick-out. The shadow was there, more distinguishable now, just behind the goalkeeper as she prepared to take the kick.

The kick-out was low and a little towards the right and, even with the slight breeze, it didn't go very far. Sinéad got to the ball in front of the Glendore number six, and she passed it to Amanda, who turned to her left and kicked it over the bar with her right foot.

'Well done, Amanda,' I shouted.

'Great pass, Sinéad.'

That brought us level. Six points each.

Glendore were good, they had good players and they worked well as a team. But so did we.

I did well during the first ten minutes of the half. I got plenty of the ball and I used it well. I didn't score again during that time, but I was involved in lots of good moves and in two of our three points. My ball handling was good and assured, my passing was accurate and my decision-making was good. And all the while, my shadow was there.

I felt good.

After about ten minutes though, just as the Glendore goalkeeper was about to take a kick-out after Aoife had missed a fairly scorable opportunity, Stephen called the referee.

'Ref!'

He rolled his left hand around his right hand in order to indicate to the referee that he was making a change. My heart sank. Ciara was standing beside Stephen, jumping up and down. I braced myself, hoping that it wasn't me who was about to be called off, but knowing that it probably was. That was the arrangement.

'Shelley!' Stephen called.

Shelley looked disappointed as she started to take off her gloves and walk towards the sideline.

'Well done, Shelley,' Debbie called.

Shelley got to the sideline, to Stephen, and Stephen gave her a tracksuit top and almost pushed Ciara in the back as Ciara ran onto the field and handed a little slip of paper to the referee. I felt relieved and I felt motivated.

I continued to play well. We continued to play well. Debbie switched to the left, despite what Stephen had said at half-time. She just took it upon herself and, when I saw her moving to the left, I moved to the right.

Debbie scored two points, one from a pass that I gave her. I scored one from the right, from a hand-pass from Debbie, straight into my path, straight over the bar. We linked up well.

We all played well together though. As a team. I

linked well with Tina and with Lily in midfield, and with Sinéad and Amanda up front, as well as with Debbie. Ciara did well when she came on. She didn't score, but she got a fair bit of the ball and her passing was good. She didn't waste much.

Tina and Lily did better than they had done in the first half in midfield. Sofia kept her kick-outs away from their number eight, as Stephen had told her to, and that negated the Glendore girl's influence. She was tall and she could catch the ball but, apart from that, she didn't have a huge amount to offer.

Our defence didn't do badly. Robyn did very well at full-back, she caught everything that came her way. And Rebecca and Edel did okay. The half-backs struggled though. In fairness, the Glendore half-forwards were very good. Their number 11 was one of the best players that we had ever faced, I'd say. She was skilful and she was tough and she was unselfish. She could catch a ball over her head and she had a strong and accurate shot, and it was very difficult to dispossess her. She gave Shauna a torrid time.

I didn't notice who was on the sideline. I heard the cheering and I heard my name called a couple of times, and I knew that Mum and Charlie and Sally and Brenda and Alan were there, and Granny and Grandad probably came with Mum for the second half, and some of the girls from school probably but, to be honest, I didn't really heed their presence. I was immersed in the game. The only presence beyond the four perimeter lines of the pitch that I heeded was my shadow's. Behind the Glendore goals.

It was a really tight game. The more time went on, the tighter it got. With about ten minutes to go, the Glendore number 11 scored another point – it must have been her fifth or sixth – and brought the scores level again. Eleven points each and no goals. A couple of minutes later, Tina burst through and kicked the ball over the bar, which gave us a one point lead, 12 points to 11.

Then the Glendore number four fumbled the kick-out and Ciara got on the ball on the right. She had options, she had Debbie and Sinéad and Amanda inside her, and Tina was calling for it in the centre, but she shot, right foot. It wasn't the wrong option, the shot was on. She went close too, but the ball hit the outside of the left-hand upright and went wide.

'Unlucky Ciara,' I heard Stephen shout.

'For God's sake, Ciara,' shouted Tina.

'Come on girls,' shouted Stephen. 'Last three minutes!'

Only three minutes?

We were close. I looked back towards the goals and faced the kick-out. My shadow was still there, behind the goals, still just standing there. I still couldn't make out the features of his face, but I knew that he was still smiling.

The Glendore goalkeeper took a short kick-out, to the Glendore number two in front of us, who had moved a couple of metres ahead of Aoife. The Glendore girl hopped the ball once as Aoife chased her, and kicked the ball up the wing, her right wing, our left wing.

It was coming our way, but I thought that it was just going to be too high for me to try to catch it. I was debating whether or not I should jump anyway, when I heard Lily shout from behind me.

'Anna!'

I stayed rooted to the ground and watched as the ball went over my head. Lily and her marker, the Glendore number nine, both jumped for the ball, as did my marker, the number five. I watched as the three of them rose. They all rose together. It was never likely that one of them was going to catch it cleanly.

Lily didn't try to catch it. She went up with her closed fist and, just as the number nine got both hands on the ball, Lily punched. Her punch was solid and strong, it knocked the ball out of the Glendore girl's hands and back towards the ground. The Glendore number five, my marker, was up in the air too. I was free. The ball bounced once and landed easily in my chest. Clever Lily.

I took a touch and moved forward into the space. Solo, hop, solo. Aoife was still to my left, but she was being marked. Sinéad was to my right, also marked. Then Aoife's marker, the number two, came towards me, which left Aoife free in behind her, so I hand-passed the ball over the number two's head to Aoife. The ball bounced once, and Aoife collected it deliberately and looked up.

The number six went towards Aoife, which left me free, and Sinéad probably free to my right. Sinéad and I both called for the ball.

'Aoife!'

Aoife hand-passed it towards us. The number six almost got a touch to it, she stretched out her left hand when the ball was in mid-air, but she just missed it. The ball was low, it landed on the ground just by my feet. I hate those ones. You don't know whether to try to get to the ball before it hits the ground, or to let it half-bounce on the ground and try to collect it as it comes back up, just off the ground.

I stooped and, as I stooped, I decided on the latter. The ball hit the ground at my feet, just before it hit my hand, but thankfully I was able to gather it quickly. It just bounced well for me. I was on the 21 now, the point was there for the taking, but we had numbers and we had their defence stretched.

Amanda was to my left, but she was marked. Sinead called for the ball to my right but, as she did, another Glendore girl, probably Debbie's marker, closed her down. That left Debbie fairly free in behind.

I hand-passed the ball over Sinéad's head, over the Glendore girl's head, and it bounced on the ground. Ciara and her marker both went for it, but Debbie was faster. She got there just in front of the pair of them and palmed the ball forward with her right hand. The ball bounced lowly on the ground, almost rolled, but Debbie stooped and had it in her hands before the Glendore goalkeeper could get to it.

The goalkeeper stretched out her arms to her right to try to block Debbie's shot, but Debbie didn't shoot. She dummied to her right, side-stepped to her left and hopped the ball, all at the same time. She was so fast, Debbie. So skilful. That left the goalkeeper sprawling on the ground on the edge of her box, and it left Debbie with an empty net. Nobody around her. Just Debbie, the ball and the open net. That must have been some feeling.

I celebrated there and then. I had punched the air while Debbie still had the ball in her hands. She dropped the ball onto her left foot and poked it. The ball trundled along the ground towards the goals. The ground was uneven, and it bobbled. You could have counted the rolls if you had wanted. You could have counted the number of times the O'Neill's logo appeared, then disappeared, then appeared again.

Then suddenly, out of nowhere, the Glendore number two appeared from the left, and she dived. She dived along the ground and she stretched out her left arm. It was a close-run thing, it was close enough to make you stop and stare in horror for a fraction of a second, she made a valiant effort but, in truth, it never really looked like she was going to get there.

Eventually, after what seemed like an age, the ball got to the goal line, rolled gently over it and nestled in the back of the net.

Pandemonium. Sinéad screamed. Aoife almost jumped on top of Amanda. Ciara jumped up and down like a possessed person. Debbie just punched the air, a little punch, and smiled. She gave me a thumbs-up sign as she made her way back to the right side of the pitch.

'Great pass.'

We weren't there yet, but we were nearly there. One or two minutes to go, and four points ahead. Glendore needed to score twice, a goal and a point at least, if they were going to even draw.

The kick-out came my way and I tried to focus. I jumped high and I stretched. I kept my eye on the ball and I stretched my legs and my back and my neck and my arms. I watched the ball as it hit my outstretched hands, directly above my head and I gripped. The ball stuck. I landed on the ground with the ball in my hands.

I felt contact from the Glendore girl after I landed, but I moved forward and I burst through. I was in the clear, Amanda to my left and Sinéad to my right when the ref blew for a free.

Which way? I hadn't done anything wrong, I surely hadn't fouled anybody, so why would he give a free against me? And why would he give me a free, if he deemed the Glendore girl's tackle to be unfair? I had the ball, I was moving forward, surely he should give me the advantage?

I looked at the ref, about to protest, regardless of which way he gave the free. But he was giving it no way. He stretched out his arms and pointed his index fingers away from his body, and he blew his whistle again. Another short, sharp phewp. He almost had his eyes closed in concentration. And again. A third time. Slightly longer.

Pheeeeeeewwwwwwwp!

The final whistle. Really?

Chapter 30

FAVOURITE SOCKS

Everything went quiet. It was really over. Everything went into slow motion.

I just stood there, motionless, powerless, still clutching the ball in my hands. I could hear the shouts, but they sounded distant, like they were miles away. Not part of my world. The county final. County champions.

I looked at the goals, beyond the goals. The shadow was still there. Daddy. The way that his shoulders were moving, it looked like he was clapping his hands in front of his body. And he was smiling. Ear to ear.

Suddenly, somebody was on my back and screaming in my ear. I wasn't expecting that, it nearly knocked me over, but I managed to remain upright, even if I did drop the ball.

'County champions!' Amanda was screaming.

Ciara arrived in front of me and Aoife arrived beside me from the left and Sinead arrived from my right. We all threw our arms around each other and everyone started jumping.

'Ballymarra! Ballymarra! Ballymarra!'

'You were great Ciara,' shouted Amanda.

'You were great too!' Ciara shouted back.

'We were all great!'

Amanda and Ciara fell to the ground and, if you didn't know better, you would have said that they were fighting. They were laughing and they were crying and they were shrieking. Sinéad was on her hunkers about five metres away, she was on her own, obviously gathering her own thoughts, allowing the achievement sink in. Or she was before Aoife ran over to her and jumped on top of her and knocked her to the ground.

Debbie and Lily had their arms around each other when Shelley joined them. Debbie saw me and stretched out her right arm, so I ran towards them and joined in. I couldn't stop smiling,

'You were brilliant Anna,' Debbie said.

'You were brilliant too,' I said.

'Your goal at the end,' I said. 'That was class. And it wasn't just your goal. You were just brilliant all around.'

'So were you,' Debbie said. 'You're a great player, Anna.'

Shelley started cheering. Lily started cheering. The four of us just flailed around in a sort of circle, cheering, jumping, arms in arms in arms in arms.

It was some feeling. The camaraderie. The friendship. All in it together. The achievement. What we achieved, we achieved it together. Champions of the county. As a team. Everybody working towards a common goal. Everybody a part of it.

The feeling of belonging to something important. I hadn't had that feeling for a long time.

Suddenly I felt an extra weight on my shoulders.

'Well done, girls!'

Stephen had joined us, and he had managed to put his long arms around the four of us.

'You were fantastic! You were all fantastic!'

We cheered and jumped up and down, and Lily ruffled Stephen's hair and Shelley jumped up on his back.

I saw Patrick, just standing there, close to the sideline, not in the middle of the pitch for some reason, staying in the background as usual, beside the dug-out, with a woman, probably his wife, and a small baby, probably a girl, probably their daughter. Or son. You can never tell with babies. He was smiling and looking at me.

'Well done, Anna,' he mouthed.

'Thanks, Patrick,' I mouthed back. 'Well done your-self!'

He probably got the 'Thanks, Patrick', part, but I'm not sure if he got the 'Well done yourself' bit.

Then I couldn't see him anymore, because Robyn and Rebecca were hurtling towards me. They joined in the jumping and the cheering until we all got tired and stopped and looked at each other, laughing, breathless.

I saw Tina, about five metres away from us. She was just there, with Sinéad and Edel. Just the three of them. They weren't jumping around, they may have already done all that. They were just standing there, as if they were waiting for a bus. I ran over to them.

'Well done, girls,' I said.

'Well done, Anna,' said Sinéad.

'Well done, Anna,' said Edel.

They were both smiling. I wasn't sure if Tina was smiling or not. She looked at me. I wasn't sure what she was going to say. It was difficult to read her expression. For a horrible moment, I thought that she was going to box me in the face. Retribution. But she didn't.

She extended her right hand. That was strange. All

the shouting and cheering and Tina wanted to shake my hand. Fair enough. I shook it. As I did though, she dragged me towards her with her right hand and she threw her left arm around my neck. And as she did that, she whispered in my ear.

'You were great today.'

I muttered something like, 'So were you.' I looked her in the eye. She was definitely smiling. Then somebody jumped on my back.

'Yaaaaaaaaaayyyyyyyy!' Sally screamed as she wrapped her legs around my stomach and her arms around my neck. 'That was awesome! You were awesome! Unbelievable! Incredible! And did I say awesome?!'

I staggered forward but managed to remain upright. Sally's brilliant. She was more excited than she would have been if she had scored the winning goal.

'Sal!'

I spun around and she fell off my back. Then she threw herself at me, front-on, and flung her arms around my neck again. As she did, I saw Sally's mum behind her, just standing there, holding little Alan by the hand, and beaming.

'Thanks so much for coming, Brenda,' I managed to say, despite the fact that her daughter was almost strangling me.

'Aw, Anna, you were brilliant. Your mum is so proud of you. I'm sure your dad is up there cheering.'

She looked to the sky. Maybe she expected me to look to the sky too, but I didn't. I wanted to say something to Brenda, thanks or something, but I didn't really know what to say. That Daddy was looking after me for sure? That I knew that? I felt the emotion surge through my stomach and into my throat. I just smiled at Brenda. I couldn't speak. Strange when deep-down sadness and sky-high euphoria meet.

Where was Mum?

Sally got off me and held me by the shoulders.

'Are you okay, Anna?'

I nodded sharply and smiled. I could feel the tears welling up in my eyes, and I was sure that Sally could see them. She looked at me sadly, and just pulled me towards her by the shoulders. I buried my head in her shoulder and concentrated on getting my tears under control.

'Where's Anna's mummy?' I heard Alan's little voice ask.

'She's here,' said Brenda.

There was a pause as Alan probably thought about it. I pulled my head away from Sally's shoulder. She looked at me and smiled.

'And where's her daddy?' asked Alan.

There was a little bit of an awkward silence.

'My daddy isn't here anymore, Alan,' I said quietly. I found my voice. 'He died a couple of years ago. He was the best daddy. But he's still with me. He will always be with me. In here.'

I pointed to my heart.

'He used to come to all my matches. He was always there. It didn't matter where the match was, or what the weather was like, he would always be there, and because he was there, I always felt confident that I would play well.'

Alan looked captivated.

'Here, I'll tell you a secret,' I said as I crouched down beside him.

'Do you like secrets?'

Alan nodded enthusiastically.

I folded down the top of the green sock on my left leg to reveal the top of my orange sock. Alan's face lit up, as if he had just seen a magic trick.

'You see these orange socks?'

Alan nodded slowly, perhaps uncertain of what might jump out of the orange socks.

'My daddy gave me these orange socks on the day that he died. He told me that, when I wore these socks,

I would play my best football. And he was right. Now, when I wear these socks in a game, he's with me. He's there. I see him.'

Alan looked up from the socks to my eyes.

'Do you believe that?' I asked.

He nodded energetically again.

'It's true. I see him.'

I stood up and looked down towards the goals. The shadow was still there. That was strange. Strange that he was still there, this long after the match had ended, and strange that I expected him to be still there.

Even stranger, Mum was down there. Behind the goals, just to the left of the goals. Nobody around her. Just Mum and the shadow. It appeared that she was looking at the shadow. I left Alan and Sally and Brenda, I mumbled something like, there's Mum, and I started walking slowly down towards the goals.

Nobody came with me or jumped on top of me or did a cartwheel in front of me. There may have been people on the pitch in front of me, but I couldn't see them. All I could see was Mum and the shadow.

And the strangest thing. As I got closer to the goals, closer to the shadow, the shape became more defined. The outline of his body became less blurred. I could see where his body ended and where the sky began. As

I drew even closer, I could make out the outline of his arm against his body. His face was still featureless, but I could just about make out where his sleeve ended and where his hand began. I thought that I could see the collar of his shirt, the belt on his jeans.

He had never been so vivid before.

I stopped walking. I was only about ten metres away now. Very close. It seemed that Mum hadn't noticed me yet. I felt scared, but safe at the same time. Scared at something that I didn't understand, but safe that, whatever it was, it was a link to Daddy.

I missed him so much.

And as I stood there, just looking at the shadow, oblivious to everything else that was going on around me, his body started to come into focus. His hands, the buttons on his shirt, his hair. And then, his face. Daddy's face. His eyes and his nose and his lips, and the lines on his cheeks. I had tried so hard to remember his face. A shiver went up my spine and through my throat so that I had to choke back the tears.

He was looking at Mum and he was smiling. His closed-mouthed smile. Just as I had imagined all this time.

I was afraid to move. I didn't want to do anything that might disturb him. I nearly didn't want him to notice me.

But he did. He turned his head and looked at me. Mum turned her head too. Her eyes were red and there were streams running down her cheeks, but she was smiling. Daddy smiled his wide open-mouthed smile.

'He has to go, pet,' Mum said.

'No!' I shouted as I ran to Daddy.

I stopped before I got to him though. He was fading again. The shadow was becoming a shadow again.

'Close your eyes, pet,' Mum said as she grabbed my hand.

I did. I just stood there and closed my eyes. I could feel the slight breeze in my face and I could feel Mum's right hand, clasped tightly against my left hand. Then I felt it. Daddy's two hands on either side of my face, half-covering my ears. It was an amazing feeling. I felt warm, comforted, safe. Then I felt his soft kiss on my forehead.

'Do your best. That's all you can do.'

I just stood there. I couldn't remember the last time I had felt this warm and safe. I thought of the morning that he sat on my bed and gave me my orange socks, and told me that he'd be home for dinner and that we could go out and play football on the green after dinner.

I allowed myself sink into the moment, his hands on

my head, his kiss on my forehead. I didn't want it to end. I didn't want him to leave.

Slowly, I felt his soft grip on my head loosen and his kiss on my forehead soften until I wasn't sure whether or not I could feel them anymore. I kept my eyes closed, shut tight, hoping that I would feel them again, but I didn't. I opened my eyes, and he was gone. The shadow was gone.

It was just me and Mum, she holding my hand more tightly than she had ever held it before, me not wanting her to let go, not ever. Tears streaming down her face. Tears streaming down my face.

We looked each other in the eyes. Sad eyes, but happy eyes. And she looked down at my right leg, where the top of my green sock was still folded down, still revealing the top of my orange sock.

'Hey, nice socks,' she said.

'Thanks,' I said. 'They're my favourite socks.'

TURN THE PAGE TO SEE THE BOOKS IN THE

GREAT IRISH SPORTS STARS SERIES

FROM THE O'BRIEN PRESS

GREAT IRISH SPORTS STARS
CORA STAUNTON

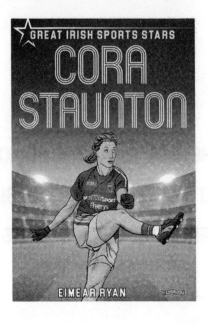

Cora could feel every nerve in her body sparking. She told herself she wasn't nervous; she was just ready for action. When she pulled on her brand-new jersey, she knew it was now or never.

Elite sportswoman Cora Staunton has always had to prove her worth: to the boys on her under-12 team, to the Mayo seniors who took a chance on her at age thirteen, and most importantly, to herself. From Croke Park to the stadiums of Sydney, Cora has become a master of the game. This is the story of how a young football-mad girl became a living legend.

GREAT IRISH SPORTS STARS
COLM 'GOOCH' COOPER

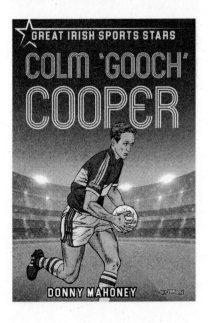

You need a boot to kick and hands and shoulders to mark your opposition. But without a sharp brain, you'll never make it as a Kerry footballer.

Follow Colm from his days as a tiny, freckle-faced kid – the youngest of five in a GAA-mad family from Killarney – all the way to Croke Park, where he won 5 All-Ireland titles. This is the story of how a boy who everyone said wasn't big enough or strong enough to wear the green and gold jersey of Kerry became one of the greatest Gaelic footballers of all time.

obrien.ie